The Definition of *K.A.R.M.A*

By:

Veronica Patrice

PaperCut

Publishing Inc.

This book is a work of fiction. Except for passing reference to real celebrities, all characters are entirely imagined and any resemblance to real persons or events is purely coincidental. Although reference is made to real celebrities, their dialogue, actions and context in which they are portrayed are all products of the author's imagination.

PaperCut Books may be purchased for educational, business or sales promotional use. For more information please write: Special Markets Department, PaperCut Publishing Inc. at veronica.patrice@ymail.com.

First Edition

Cover Designed by Veronica Patrice
Interior text designed by Veronica Patrice

Library of Congress Cataloging-in-Publication Data

Veronica Patrice
The Definition of *KARMA*/ by Veronica Patrice._1st Edition

ISBN: 978-0-578-02850-7

I dedicate this book to everyone that has been cheated on, lied to or betrayed. It may be difficult to see the lining in the sky but hold on because K.A.R.M.A is a BITCH!!

Acknowledgments

First and foremost I would like to thank God for he has given me the strength to press on when I honestly felt I had no reason to. Next, I would like to thank my Mommy because you are the epitome of what a mom is and I am so proud to be your daughter. I may be a daddy's girl but I am still my mommy's sweetie. Daddy, I truly appreciate you and you always seem to think of me first even when you are going through so much. I love you both and thanks for always being there!!!

Before I go any further I must thank everyone for purchasing "my baby", *All That Glitters* and making it such a success. I would have never believed that my writing could have opened so many doors. Your support and encouragement motivates me and I sincerely hope that you enjoy this second effort.

To my cousin Sheree, I thank you for holding me down at CWD; I would not have made it without you. You are truly an inspiration and I wish you much success in every venture you attempt. Don't forget we're still going to Paris!! So get moving on this trilogy, My Soul on Paper III.

To my little sisters Nichole and Nadine I love you and no more babies please. (WAIT!!) The both of you keep doing big things!!

To Lamere, Laquira (a.k.a. Kay Kay), Terrance (a.k.a. Lemuel), Titus (my Snickers) and Tyrell I love you. You all are growing up so fast but I know you all will grow up to be strong and successful.

Keisha, Keisha we sometimes see things differently but blood is always thicker than water. So no matter what decisions we make in our lives I will always love you. Thanks for always being there no matter what and never passing judgment. It's time to celebrate margaritas on me. Ha!!!

As a whole I would like to thank the rest of my family because just trying to name half of you is a book within itself. To all of my friends I love and appreciate each of you.

Shouts out to Big Boy for being one of the coolest dudes I have ever known. Even though we beef sometimes its all love. Steve, I thank you for being my best friend even though we do not see eye to eye most of the time. You will always have a piece of my heart.

Fat Boy Slim, I thank you so much for just being there and believing in me. You have been a better friend than you will ever know. I truly appreciate that no matter what you are always there. Good looking homie!!!

If I did not mention your name please blame my mind and not my heart. And last but not least I would like to give a special thank you to everyone who purchased this book. I sincerely thank for your support and remarks but stay tuned because this show has just begun.

State of Affairs

"Everybody down on the ground and no one gets hurt!" yelled the robber.

As Karma kneeled down onto the frigid, damp floor she wondered what else could go wrong today. It began with her oversleeping and then she broke her heel trying to catch the train in an attempt to make it to work on time. A failed attempt because she was still forty five minutes late but fortunately her boss was not upset.

She frantically ran into his office to make up some colossal explanation for her tardiness.

As Karma approached his desk she said, "Mr. Stockman I have a legitimate explanation."

Before Karma could finish her lie he interrupted and said, "Its ok there's no need for an explanation."

"Thank you for understanding and I promise this will never happen again."

Karma was about to leave then unexpectedly Mr. Stockman asked her to have a seat at the round table next to his desk. She walked over to the table and took a seat. He then walked over to his desk and picked up a stack of papers. *Great some more work Karma thought.*

As Karma patiently waited for him to reach the table he said, "You're an exceptional worker and I feel honored to be your employer but our profits this quarter were not what we expected. I wanted to talk to you because you were rewarded with a considerably large raise last month." I know they're not trying to take back my raise Karma thought silently as he continued.

"We appreciate all of your hard work but we can no longer afford your salary." he said cautiously.

I can't believe this bullshit! I have worked here for over two fucking years with no raise. Now a month after I finally get a raise you want to take it back. No fuck that this is straight bullshit! Was what Karma wanted to say but she could not afford to lose her job.

Karma was a Fashion Public Relations (PR) Specialist at Jones New York in the heart of Chicago. It was not the best paying job but it kept her bills paid and she enjoyed it. Karma started out with a moderate salary of $43,000 but worked her way up the corporate ladder. She was now pulling in close to $60,000 a year.

Even though Karma was boiling on the inside she calmly said, "I'm very disappointed that there's no other recourse besides a demotion since I was really enjoying this position. I also enjoyed my previous position which is good since I have to go back to it." Karma said with slight smile.

Mr. Stockman appeared to be confused. The two sat in silence for awhile until he walked over and put his hand on Karma's shoulder.

"I think you may have misunderstood what I said. I am truly sorry but we can no longer afford your new salary or your previous salary. I apologize for the short notice but today will be your last day."

Karma sat in complete shock as he continued, "We have put together a very generous severance package and I insist that you list me as a reference. But unfortunately at this time there's nothing further I can do for you. Hopefully things will pick up and when they do you'll be the first person I call." he said seemingly pleased with himself.

"Bullshit," Karma screamed. "How the fuck could you afford to give me a raise last month but this month you can't even afford to pay me?"

"Please calm down I do not want to have to call security," he threatened.

Karma animatedly stood up and said, "Fuck that call security because this is bullshit. You just talked all of this bullshit about how great of an employee I am just to fire me."

She snatched her check and said "You could've called me at home for this bullshit and sent me my damn check in the mail."

"I am truly sorry but please don't make this any worst than it has to be." he said as security walked in.

"I hope that you sleep well tonight because karma is a BITCH!" Karma said before pushing through the scrawny flash light security officers.

Karma went to retrieve her things from her office. She grabbed a picture of her and her best friend on vacation and some other pictures from her desk. She placed her belongings into her black tote then grabbed her purse from her drawer. Karma thought about taking some other things such as her plants and other knick knacks but decided against it. Before walking out she glanced over her office and it finally hit her that she no longer had a job. Karma turned around and walked toward the elevators.

Her coworkers sat in silence not sure of what to say or do. The last thing they wanted was for her to go off and kill everyone. Karma ignored them as she waited for the elevator. When the elevator doors opened she looked back and everyone just stared at her. She just turned back around and entered the elevator.

After she reached the main lobby she walked through the revolving doors and was met by a chilly wind gust. Karma was accustomed to the cold being that she was born and raised in Chicago. As Karma walked toward the train station she decided to open her last check. She suddenly stopped mid-step and her mouth dropped at the number of zeros. It was a check made out to her for the amount of $15,000.

Karma immediately hailed a cab and made her way to Chicago Community Bank on 35th Street. Karma kept replaying how foolishly she had acted towards her boss when he was actually trying to help her. The more she thought about it the more she wanted to hurry and get to the bank. Karma wanted to make it to the bank before her boss changed his mind and put a stop payment on the check.

The cab driver pulled up to the curb directly facing Chicago Community Bank. She paid the cab driver then made her way inside of the bank. Karma stood in the shortest line with only two people ahead of her. As the line began moving forward the man in front of her suddenly turned around. He immediately pulled two large handguns from his waist.

"Everybody down on the ground and no one gets hurt," yelled the robber.

As Karma kneeled down onto the frigid, damp floor she wondered where the hell security was now.

"Shut the fuck up and put the money in the bag." the robber said interrupting her thoughts.

"I'm sorry, I have a husband and three kids please don't kill me," the terrified bank teller pleaded as she fulfilled the robber's request.

"Freeze!" screamed the police officer. "This is the Chicago police put your weapon down and your hands up where I can see them!"

The robber panicked and shot the bank teller four times at point blank range. He then peeled Karma's lifeless body off of the floor and proceeded to place the gun to her right temple. It was still warm from the bullets he had just released. Suddenly at that moment Karma realized not having a job was the least of her worries.

"Back up or the bitch dies!" the robber screamed.

"Look we have the building surrounded. You can either walk out of here in hand cuffs or you can be rolled out of here inside of a body bag. If you let the woman go you still have options. Everyone makes mistakes but you have to let the hostages' go." the police officer pleaded.

"Fuck that I ain't going back I'll kill this bitch before I go back," the robber screamed while tightening the grip his forearm had around Karma's neck.

"Killing her isn't going to solve anything it will only make matters worst. It's not worth it man let these innocent people go." the cop said trying to bargain with the robber.

With Karma's life in limbo she wondered if the real negotiator was ever going to show up. The cop was nothing like Samuel L. Jackson who was just acting in a movie.

Karma could barely breathe because of the tight grasp the robber had around her neck. He was at least six feet tall somewhat heavy but he was still ripped in all of the right places. The robber was kind of cute but what kind of robber does not wear a mask. He had to be an amateur Karma thought because he could not even hold his gun steady. At that point Karma kept going in and out of consciousness but the last thing she remembered was a loud BANG!

On the other side of town Asia sat up from her nap and the clock read 4:19. *Damn it!* It was the forth night this week that Jay had not come home. It was now 4 o'clock in the damn afternoon and Jay was still not home. He had left to go to the store last night around eleven but he always had some story as to why he did not make it back. Asia was tired of this shit. She could not understand why Jay did not respect her. She did not mind him acting this way when she was stripping but now she was pregnant with his first born. The least he could do was come home at a decent hour she thought. She decided to wait for him downstairs because today she was determined to get an explanation. As she opened the bedroom door to go downstairs she was startled by an intoxicated Jay.

"Where the fuck you been at? You think you can just walk in here anytime. I'm so tired of this shit you don't even have the decency to be discreet. You walk in here still reeking of pussy from last night but I'm not supposed to be mad." Asia yelled.

"Asia chills the fuck out you always on that bullshit." Jay said nonchalantly.

Jay continued to ignore Asia as he walked toward the bathroom to take a shower. He had to admit she was right because it was time for him to stop treating her like that. He realized that no matter how he looked at it Asia was still three months pregnant. Jay still could not understand why she was always trippin'.

Jay met Asia about six months ago. She was a stripper at this club called, Naughty Girl. Asia was fine as hell and was easily the baddest bitch in there. She was about 5'6 with a petite frame and a fat ass. You could probably sit a bottle on her ass and she would not notice.

As Jay walked into the club Asia was dancing on stage to the Ying Yang Twins; Shake it Like a Salt Shaker. She had every man fascinated by the way she flipped her body upside down on the pole all the while making it clap. It was like she had these men hypnotized because within minutes they were emptying their wallets onto the stage.

Strip clubs were not Jay's style but it was where he conducted most of his business. That night he was meeting with this old head named Slim. He owned a lot of real estate throughout Chicago and was going to help Jay turn legit.

Slim had come up as a street hustler too but he was one of the lucky ones that did not get burned by the game. He told Jay a few years back to contact him when he was ready to move on. Back then Jay felt like he was on top of the world but now the game had changed.

No one was loyal everyone wanted to play the game but no one wanted to suffer the consequences. Jay knew that it was time for him to get out of the game. He knew these young cats did not stand for nothing meaning they would fall for anything. And once they had fallen they would bring him down next.

As Jay waited for Slim he noticed a very sexy woman approaching him. She looked like brown sugar especially the way the lights glistened off of her body. She had a petite waist but was thick everywhere else. Her long, black, curly hair just bounced as she stared into Jay's eyes. She had light brown eyes but the lights made them appear to be green or grey.

She stood in front of Jay's table and asked, "Would you like a dance?"

While slowly removing his tooth pick he replied, "I don't like being teased so no thank you."

She seemed to be taken aback by his response. The sexy woman proceeded to climb on top of the table. She then jumped into Jay's lap while simultaneously pushing the table back.

"I promise not to tease if you promise to please." she whispered.

Jay was slightly intrigued by her response but not completely because she was a stripper. He told her he had some business to handle but they could hook up later.

The sexy woman hopped off of Jay's lap and went to solicit some more lap dances. Jay stood up and began walking toward the back where Slim's office was located. Standing a few feet from his door were two muscle bound security guards but these were not your average metro security flash light cops. The guard on the right was dark skinned with braids. He was about 6'5 and had to be at least 350 pounds. His partner was light skinned with a bald head and a tattoo that covered the entire right side of his head. As Jay walked toward the door both men gave him their undivided attention.

"I'm here to see Slim." Jay said as he reached the door.

"Who you?" the guard with the tattoo asked.

Before Jay could respond the office door opened and Slim stepped out. He had that old school swagger like pimps had back in the day. He was decked out in light blue slacks creased to perfection and a white short sleeved button down with matching blue stripes.

"Ahh man how you doin," Slim said as him and Jay embraced each other.

"Aye my people didn't rough you up too much did they?" he laughed while jokingly patting his guard on the back.

"Slim you know how we do." the guard countered while smiling.

"I know that's what I pay you for but it ain't no need for that because this man right here. This man right here is my prodigy." Slim explained to the guards.

"He reminds me a lot of myself when I was young and dumb. I made a lot of money back then but I was hardheaded just like this one. I wish I would've had someone take me under their wing before I self-destructed." Slim said before entering his office as Jay followed.

"It looks like you run a tight ship." Jay said as he sat down in the chair across from his desk.

"Yeah but they were just headstrong knuckle heads in the trap like you. They're a little rough around the edges but they are for the most part good guys. The one with the tat is Cutty and the other is AJ." Slim explained.

"Well let's cut the chase and get down to business." Slim said and Jay agreed.

A Twist of Fate

As Asia danced her eyes landed on this cat she knew had some major chips. She was into him the moment she saw him stroll into the club. Asia was dancing on the stage but oddly he seemed not to notice. Usually when she hit the stage it was all eyes on her even the other dancers were captivated by her moves. After her set was complete she went to approach him but he still appeared to be uninterested. He must have been misinformed because Asia a.k.a. Cinnamon always got what she wanted.

Mister tall, dark and handsome was dressed in a red Armani button down with some dark blue Red Monkey jeans. He had a low fade and his beard was lined to perfection. Asia needed that piece of chocolate so she offered to give him a lap dance.

"I don't like being teased so no thank you." he said.

What, who does he think he is telling me no Asia questioned. I am Cinnamon, I am the baddest bitch in here and he says no thank you. Maybe he's one of those homo thugs she thought.

There was only one way to find out Asia thought before leaping into his lap. He was straight alright because as soon as her fat ass hit his middle someone became very happy. He was definitely working with something and Asia intended to find out.

The club was about to close and Asia still had not heard anything from tall, dark and handsome. She waited a little while longer but there was still no sign of him. Asia eventually made her way to the parking lot but as she was walking a white Cadillac Escalade with dark tint cut her off. She was about to go off but as the window rolled down she realized it was tall, dark and handsome.

"I thought we were hooking up tonight," he questioned.

"What you're done handling your business," she said casually.

"Yeah, why don't you jump in so we can get out of here?" he said while turning his head as if he already knew her answer.

"What about my car? It'll get towed if I leave it up here." Asia said appearing to be concerned but truthfully she could care less about that car. It was a semi-new Corolla but it had nothing on the stock she was about to invest in.

"I'll have someone pick it up and bring it to you later?"

Without answering him she walked over to the passenger side and climbed into the truck.

"So what's your name shorty?" he asked as he pulled off.

"Cinnamon and yours," she replied.

"Chocolate," he said jokingly.

"Well let me taste it and see," she said as she leaned over the console.

Asia began unbuckling his belt. She then unbuttoned his pants and his friend greeted her. She slowly grabbed it and did what she did best.

"Yeah eat that dick girl," he said as he swerved through the lanes.

"You want some chocolate don't you," he asked.

Asia looked up into his eyes with her mouth completely filled and said, "Yes daddy give mommy some chocolate."

That was all she wrote because within minutes he grabbed her hair and held her head down as he released himself into her mouth. Asia lifted her head, licked her lips and swallowed all of him. As his cum dripped down her throat she knew he was putty in her hand even though she still did not know his name.

Asia cleaned up as he drove to the motel down the street. Jay was at least eleven inches with stamina for days. He put it on Asia so good that she could not remember how many orgasms she had actually had.

As Jay slept next to her she began thinking of what scam she could run on him. She thought about running the whole I'm pregnant routine to get a few dollars for an abortion. But she realized that Jay had more than just money he actually had a heart. If she could get pregnant he would probably want to settle down and get married especially if she were carrying his first child. From that day Asia knew Jay was going to be a definite long-term investment.

Jay and Asia had been seeing each other for almost six months. Asia was now three months pregnant so Jay believed. They were never in a relationship per say but after Asia told him she was pregnant he moved her into his place. This was a definite upgrade since they were technically just, "fuck buddies."

Initially when Asia moved in with Jay he promised to clean up his act but nothing had changed. He was still in the streets and he was still sexing other women. She even agreed that he could still sleep with other women as long as she was apart of it. But that still was not good enough.

"Ahhhhh," Asia screamed as a sharp pain shot through her stomach.

Asia was almost beginning to believe her own lies. The stress was beginning to take a toll on her mentally and physically. Asia began developing real feelings for Jay; he was no longer just another john to her.

Asia began to climb into their bed when she felt another sharp pain but this time she fell to the ground. Multiple pains began to shoot through her body simultaneously.

Asia remained on the floor in the fetal position with tears vigorously running down her face as she screamed, "Jay!"

"Oh my god where am I, what happened to me?" Karma asked herself.

Feeling completely out of it her mind began to wander as she tried to remember what had happened. Her thoughts were quickly interrupted when the nurse walked in.

"You're finally awake how do you feel?" the perky nurse asked.

"I don't know what happened to me, how did I get here?"

"Honey you are at Luke Memorial Hospital. You were shot in the stomach during a bank robbery and we had to perform emergency surgery. You are very lucky because the bullet just grazed your spinal cord. We have been really worried about you because you've been in a coma for over a week. I need to examine you to make sure you are healing properly. Do you feel up to it or would you like me to come back a little later?" the concerned nurse asked.

"If you don't mind could you come back later this is still a lot for me to take in." Karma stated still somewhat confused.

"No problem honey my name is Maryann and if you need anything just push this red button." she said before walking out.

Karma was still in disbelief that she had been shot in a bank robbery. As she rested she began remembering bits and pieces about the day of the shooting. Suddenly she remembered the check for $15,000 and also about being fired. Everything was slowly coming back to her but one thing she did not forget was her best friend Angel. She reached over for the phone and her body ached as if she was a hundred years old. Karma picked up the receiver and dialed her best friend.

"Hello!" Angel said as her music blared in the background.

"Hey girl," Karma said.

"Oh my god Karma is that you?" Angel screamed as the music came to an immediate halt.

"Yeah girl I'm in the hospital I was shot during a bank robbery last week they said I've been in a coma ever since."

“Oh my god Karma, I’ve been worried sick what hospital are you at?”

“Luke Memorial Hospital but I’m not sure where I feel really out of it.” Karma said looking around trying to find a room number or something.

“Ok, Karma I’m just leaving work and its rush hour but I’ll be there as soon as I can.”

“Ok Angel I’ll see you when you get here.

After they hung up Karma reminisced about everything they had been through over the years. Karma questioned herself as to where she would be without Angel?

“What the hell is wrong with you?” Jay screamed.

Since there was no answer Jay assumed Asia was just trying to get some attention so he continued with his shower. By the time he walked into the bedroom he found Asia unconscious on the floor in a pile of her own blood. Jay rushed to the phone and dialed 911 but they immediately placed him on hold.

Ain't this some bullshit, the police are never around when you want them to be Jay silently thought.

Jay hung up the phone then reached down and picked Asia up into his arms. He carried an unconscious Asia to his car. She had already lost a lot of blood Jay kept regretting not going down stairs when he heard her first scream.

Jay finally pulled up to Luke Memorial Hospital and jumped out of the car. He ran to the passenger side and carried Asia inside of the hospital. The doctors immediately grabbed her and put her on a stretcher. He sat in the waiting room covered in blood feeling that this entire situation was his fault. His thoughts were soon interrupted when a familiar face walked through the door.

"Angel is that you?" Jay asked.

"Oh my God, Jay is you ok?" she asked looking over his blood stained clothing.

"I'm ok but ahh my friend is here." he stuttered.

"Oh ok…. well I hope they're doing ok but I gotta go. You remember Karma don't you? She was the girl you swore you were going to marry all through school. Well she was shot and has been in a coma I'm going to see her right now. She's been in here for over a week but the hospital couldn't find a next of kin."

"Damn I remember Karma how can I forget I was so in love with her and she didn't even know it. I hope she's ok, give her my sympathy and by the way it was really nice seeing you. Do you mind if we exchange numbers and maybe hookup under better circumstances?"

Angel and Jay exchanged numbers then went their separate ways. Jay sat back down in the waiting area and wondered what was going to happen with Asia. He felt guilty for not knowing any of her family or friends but it was too late. Truthfully he really did not know Asia even though she is or was the mother of his first child. As he gazed over his blood stained clothing he wondered if his child's blood was really on his hands. Putting his thoughts behind him Jay decided to see if there were any updates regarding Asia.

"Excuse me; I want to know the status of Asia Buchanan. I've been here for almost three hours and I still haven't heard anything?" Jay asked noticeably irritated.

"Sir she's still in surgery as soon as I have some information I will let you know. By the way would you like some clean clothes they aren't fancy but they are clean?" the nurse suggested.

"Sure but please let me know as soon as you know something."

"I sure will," she said as she handed him some hospital scrubs.

"If you would like to wash up you're welcome to. Just take this elevator up to the second floor and then follow the blue line on the floor. When you get to the red line make a right. The first three rooms should be available. You can relax for awhile and if I hear anything regarding Ms. Buchanan I will let you know."

"Thank you so much Miss," Jay said slightly taken aback by her hospitality.

As Jay waited for the elevator he began reminiscing about the last time he had seen Karma. That was a very special night for him. Not only because it was prom but it was the first and last time he and Karma made love.

Once Jay arrived on the second floor he went into the first available room. Jay immediately peeled the bloody clothing from his body and jumped into the steamy hot shower. After showering he decided to relax before he went back to check on Asia. Jay watched TV for awhile and then eventually nodded off.

Love, Lies & Deceit

As Angel waited for the elevator she thought about what a coincidence it was running into Jay. Angel could not wait to tell Karma because she knew she would be shocked. The last time they had seen each other was at prom. Jay had asked Karma to go with him but she already had a date. It still amazed Angel that Jay still believed Karma did not know he had a crush on her. Angel believed that something else had gone on between those two but Karma swore nothing happened. She claimed that she was not attracted to Jay but Angel was almost certain that Karma had a crush as well. After Angel walked out of the elevator she walked over to the information desk.

"Excuse me," Angel said to the receptionist.

"I'm looking for Karma Simms please?"

"Hello who are you to the patient?"

"I'm her sister?" Angel replied.

"Your sister is in room 304 just follow this blue line. When you see the red line you're going to turn right and 304 should be about three doors down." the nurse directed.

"Thank you." Angel said as she walked away.

Angel knocked lightly on Karma's room door while gently turning the knob just in case she was sleeping.

"Oh my goodness Karma how are you doing?" Angel said as she ran to her bedside. Surprisingly Karma looked good especially after everything she had been through.

"I'm ok. I'm just hungry I'm tired of this bullshit they keep feeding me." Karma said as she adjusted her body trying to find a comfortable position.

Angel noticed that Karma had lost a lot of weight but she still looked like herself. Her hair was pulled up into a bun the same way she wore it around the house.

"Girl I knew you were going to be hungry so I brought you a roman burger and fries. I didn't get you a soda because I had nowhere to put it." Angel said as she handed her the food.

"Angel I love you so much" she said as she stuffed the roman burger into her mouth.

"Karma you better slow down before you choke. I know you're hungry but damn." Angel watched in amazement as Karma devoured an entire roman burger in just four bites.

After Karma finished eating she and Angel talked and talked. Before they knew it, it was a quarter after ten. By this time Angel had now become hungry so she decided to walk to the vending machines. As she walked out of the room she walked directly into Jay.

"Two times in one day," Jay said as they bumped into one another.

"I know right I was just going to get me and Karma some snacks. How's you're friend?" Angel asked while stepping back.

"I'm not sure she was in surgery but I nodded off. I'm actually on my way downstairs now to check up on her. Do you mind walking together because I really need to check on my friend? I think the vending machines are on the first floor too."

"Cool we can catch up and you can tell me who this "friend" is. You were never a good liar and all that stuttering you were doing earlier I know you're up to something." she said irrefutably.

As they walked down to the vending machines Jay told Angel what he was into and how he was trying to clean up his act. He also explained to her about Asia and the baby. Angel picked up on the fact that Jay did not want to discuss the baby so she changed the subject. Angel was very surprised that this was his first child because he was always a playboy. She did commend him on stepping up because men now and days did not.

Angel went on to tell Jay that she was married and had two kids. Jay was surprised that Angel's husband was DeMarcus. It was indeed a small world because DeMarcus and Jay were super tight growing up. They were both on the football and track team. Jay was saddened to learn DeMarcus had been gunned down a year earlier. As they walked toward the vending machines Jay made his way to the nurse's station.

"Excuse me; is Asia Buchanan out of surgery?" Jay questioned.

"She is as a matter of fact her doctor is right over there." the nurse said while pointing to the middle age white man walking in his direction.

Jay approached the doctor and asked, "Is Asia Buchanan ok how's the baby?"

"Sir, surgery went well Ms. Buchanan is now in recovery. She was treated for Dermoid Cyst of both ovaries which caused all of the blood and severe abdomen pain. I'm sorry sir but Ms. Buchanan has not and will never be able to bear children."

Jay stood there in complete awe.

"Doctor are you sure did she know that she couldn't have kids." Jay asked praying for some type of explanation.

"Oh yeah sir she's known about this since she was an adolescent. Don't worry she is recovering well and you're welcome to visit her but keep in mind she needs her rest." the doctor said before walking off.

Damn, Damn, Damn Asia thought to herself as she sat in the hospital bed. It was not supposed to happen like this or even this soon. She had planned to have the "miscarriage" in a couple of weeks. Ok, ok think positive he may feel bad enough about the miscarriage that he might want to stay Asia hoped. Well there is only one way to find out she concluded as she turned to pick up the phone Jay walked into her room.

This was not good Asia thought as she examined Jay from head to toe. She wondered if he had spent the night because he was dressed in hospital scrubs. At that point Asia knew nothing good could come of his visit.

Jay's expression was so frigid that she could feel it before he even reached her. What made her really nervous was how calm he seemed to be. He quietly walked into the room and sat next to her bed. Ten minutes had passed and he had yet spoken one word. He would not even look at her but he instead just stared at the wall. He finally looked over to Asia and went off.

"You dirty bitch! I've been sitting in this damn hospital for almost eight hours straight blaming myself for this bullshit. I've been worried as hell about you and you're going sit here and not say nothing. You're not even going to apologize?" he questioned.

"Jay what do you want me to apologize for I didn't make myself have a miscarriage. If anything this is your fault. If you weren't out in the streets all night maybe this wouldn't have happened." Asia said with little emotion.

"What baby", he screamed and before she could answer he stood up.

"Bitch you weren't never pregnant and you will never be pregnant. Why the fuck you lie? You wanted some money? You wanted me to wife you? Bitch you crazy I wouldn't wife you if you were the last bitch on an island of transvestites. Fuck you! When you get out of the hospital your shit will be in storage. There's no need to call or come see me I'll leave the key at the front desk." he said as he stormed out.

That fucking bitch! Jay was so heated that he took the stairs instead of waiting for the elevator. His mind started replaying the day's events. Her blood had drenched his clothing, car and house yet she had the nerve to try to blame him. Jay had taken care of Asia and moved her out of the projects and this is how she repaid him. Fuck her he screamed inside the empty stairwell. As Jay opened the door he caught a glimpse of Angel talking to someone. As Jay walked closer he heard someone call his name from behind. He turned around and he was now facing **KARMA**.

Second Chances

A year and a half had passed since the whole "Asia" fiasco and robbery. Karma had no clue choosing Jay would entail so much especially his "relationship" with Asia. That bitch was certifiably crazy; the state needed to issue her a check ASAP.

When Asia was released from the hospital she was dead broke, heart-broken and out for revenge. She did everything in her power to break Jay down. She even went as far as to tell the cops about some of his doings. Now you know that's low Karma could not imagine snitching on her worst enemy. But that's neither here nor there because they were both cut from a different cloth. Karma loved Jay to death but sometimes she wished she would have never gotten caught up in his shit.

Initially when Jay and Karma reunited they were just friends. They both were secretly in love with each other but neither was ready to rush into anything. They talked on the phone and went out occasionally. Quiet as kept Jay was still messing around with that crazy bitch Asia. What more can you say men can really be dumb sometimes.

Even though Jay and Karma were not official so-to-speak they were beginning to get very serious. They spoke daily and had even taken a few exotic vacations together. They had not been intimate since high school but it was getting harder and harder to keep the goodies on lock.

Unbeknown to Karma Jay was ready to take their relationship to the next level. Karma was excited when Jay called to invite her to a special dinner. Karma secretly hoped that Jay would make her his "official" girl.

It was the month of April and love was definitely in the air. Karma was floating on cloud nine. She could only hear birds chirping and see flowers sprouting. It sounds corny but Karma was ready for love. Snapping back to reality she realized she still had to get an outfit for the night as well as make her 3 o'clock hair appointment. As usual Karma put a call into her partner in crime.

"Hey girl" Karma eagerly said as she turned on the shower.

"What do you want Karma you know I don't like being woke up?" a jaded Angel asked.

"Sorry but its 8:30 shouldn't you be up already? Anyways Jay is planning this dinner for me tonight and I need a new fit so I wanted to see if you were down."

"Ok but why are you calling me so early?" Angel said still somewhat out of it.

"Because I have an appointment at Diamonds at 3:00 and you know that's going to be an all day affair." Karma said while pulling her hair into a bun.

"Yeah you right about that but what time are you trying to go? After I drop them off at daycare I'll swing over there and we can decide what's what from there. Madison has a doctor's appointment at 1 o'clock so I have to be back by then."

"That's cool I'm about to get in the shower call me when you're on your way."

"Alright" Angel said as she hung up.

"Mason, Madison breakfast is ready!" Angel screamed.

Angel loved her kids but sometimes she just needed a break. She was rapidly growing tired of everything falling on her. She had to work, cook, clean and take care of her kids' day in and day out. Sometimes she wondered if she was being punished for something she did in her past. It was not like she was a hoe or even a single parent by choice. She did not sleep around with every Tom, Dick and Harry.

Angel had two beautiful children by her husband whom she thought would always be there. DeMarcus may have still had some street connections but he was moving on from that life. Then abruptly some low life turns Angel's life upside down. She felt all alone left without a husband and her children were left without a father and for what.

Angel's thoughts were suddenly interrupted by the sound of glass shattering.

"Sorry mommy Mason pushed me." Madison whined.

"Go sit at the table and watch where you step. Yall better and stop fooling around now," Angel screamed.

"Mommy, Mommy can I have some more bacon?" Madison said while grabbing the bacon off of the plate.

"Mommy can I have some more juice?" Mason whined.

"Mommy Mason just drunk my juice," Madison shrieked.

"The both of you be quiet NOW!" Angel yelled then continued. "Madison why ask for something if you already took it? I told you about that! Mason keep your hands to yourself and since you chose not to you cannot have any more juice. Both of you hurry up and go get dressed before we are late."

Mason and Madison were already driving their mom crazy. Angel was on her last nerve as she finished cleaning up the kitchen. Before she could leave the kitchen the phone rang.

"Hello!"

"Angel what's up this Jay?"

"Oh what's up" Angel said relieved it was not someone else.

"Nothing much just trying to get this dinner together" Jay said apprehensively.

"It's just a dinner it's not like you're proposing to the girl. You guys go out all of the time what's so special about tonight?" Angel said nonchalantly.

"Man Angel I want to propose to her but I don't wanna come off soft. I really love that girl but what if she says, no?" Jay asked.

"She won't she's in love with you just as much as you are with her. What do have planned so far?" Angel asked while walking upstairs.

"Ok first I'm going to pick her up and take her to dinner somewhere classy. Then we're going to ride to the airport and take a private jet to Las Vegas. Finally I'm going to pop the question at the Garden of Gods Pool Oasis," he said excitedly.

"Damn," was all Angel could formulate.

"Hopefully we can elope that night and spend the rest of the week in Vegas for our honeymoon. So what you think Angel? Is that too much? Not enough? Say something Angel," Jay shouted.

"Damn Jay you going all out of course she's going to say yes. Oh my god I can't believe you guys are going to elope. Damn I didn't even get an invitation. I'm just speechless but it's cool though I really happy for you guys. Shit all I got is these kids and no man anyway." Angel said slightly jealous.

"Angel please you know if you wanted a man you would have one. I know you miss my mans but it's time to move on."

"On that note it's time for me to take these kids to daycare and go hook-up with your fiancé-to-be." Angel said quickly not wanting to go there.

"Whatever Angel you know I'm right but don't tell Karma anything. I mean it Angel nothing," he roared.

"Yeah, yeah alright" Angel said before hanging up.

Jay loved Karma but…..Honestly there were no buts because he knew Karma was the one for him. Seriously, who was he kidding Karma was his first and only love. Jay loved her long beautiful hair and her dark brown eyes. Her mahogany skin was as soft as silk and as rich as milk chocolate. Karma was the first girl that he actually listened to. When she spoke her lips hypnotized him and her words infatuated him. Her intelligence was so sexy and her street brilliance just ratified his love.

Jay loved the way Karma walked into a room and her mere existence would command everyone's attention. Jay did not know if it was the sway in her hips or just the confidence she exudes. Karma was full of love but there was a certain pain underneath it all that attracted Jay to her more. He wanted to be the one to heal her heart but he knew there would be no second chances if he fucked up. Jay knew if he went all of the way Asia would have to become a distant memory.

Honestly even Jay did not know why he still messed with that girl. After everything Asia had put him through he still kept going back. One reason was because Asia's head game was crazy. She shamed veterans' like Superhead without hesitation. Jay was now aware that she was unable to bear kids which meant he could go raw without getting trapped. Jay decided once and for all he was through with Asia but not before he hit it on last time.

Jay did not have much time so he hurriedly put on his shoes and headed to the garage. He jumped into his whip and headed to Stateway Garden projects. Asia lived on the south side of Chicago which limited the chances of her running into Karma.

Jay did not bother calling because he knew Asia's good for nothing ass would be home. He also knew she was not dumb enough to bring another dude into where he paid the bills. They say it ain't tricking if you got it were words Jay had come to live by. Also her rent for the year was only six hundred dollars and he could spend that in one night at the bar.

As Jay pulled up to her building he looked up and seen her lights on. He walked toward the door and was about to knock when the door opened. Asia was dressed in some pink boy shorts and a wife beater with no bra.

"Hey daddy", she said as she leaned on the door.

Just looking at her made his dick hard. Damn was he really about to give all of this up he pondered.

"What you cook for breakfast?" he asked as he walked into the house.

One thing about Asia was that she lived in the projects but you could not tell from the inside. She kept everything neat and clean.

"I ate cereal this morning but I can make you something real quick," she said as she closed the door.

"Bring me some of that sweet pussy that's what I want for breakfast." Jay said as he took a seat at the kitchen table.

Asia jumped up from the couch and removed her shorts. She jumped on the table and spread her legs wide ready for Jay to dive in. Jay always enjoyed teasing her so he gently rubbed his fingers over her clit. Just grazing it enough to make her groan and grind her hips. She began to play with her pussy sliding one finger in at a time. Jay's dick was now rock hard. He grabbed her legs and pulled them to the end of the table. Jay decided to skip four play all together and instead went in head first. Asia was the only pussy he had eaten since Karma and that was way back in high school.

"Ohh daddy right there don't stop," Asia moaned.

Jay was ready to stick something as he begun sucking on her clit. He then inserted three fingers into her pussy and like magic she came. While her pussy was still leaking he pulled her up from the table and turned her around. Jay unbuckled his belt and unbuttoned his pants letting them fall to the floor. His dick was already peeking through his boxers with pre cum oozing from its tip.

Jay forcefully pushed Asia back until her face kissed the table as he entered her pussy from behind. He drove his dick into her pussy with long, deep strokes. Jay slowly stroked her pussy wanting to savor every last drop.

"Ahh shit daddy I'm about to cum," Asia screamed.

Jay began to speed up his pace and was now driving all nine inches into her while pressing her head against the table. When he felt her juices splash onto his dick he almost lost it. Jay was about to cum but before he did he grabbed Asia by her head and pushed her to her knees. She routinely grabbed his dick and began deep throating. Jay fucked her face until his dick spat thick white cum into her face. Asia then grabbed his dick and licked it clean rubbing it against her face to get every last drop.

Humble Beginnings

Dressed and ready to go Karma sat impatiently on the couch waiting for Angel who was never on time no matter the occasion. As Karma waited she began reflecting on her life and the direction it was going. Here she was twenty-five years old with no kids, no husband and no job. She had been in college for what seemed like forever. She felt like she was going nowhere fast.

Karma was far from rich but do not get it twisted she was a far cry from broke. Karma had been on her on since she was sixteen and she did not have to strip or sell her body to pay the bills. She was a bona-fide hustler meaning she could always get money whether it was legally or illegally.

Karma Simms was born and raised on the north side of Chicago, Illinois. She grew up on a street called Evergreen which was also the home of one of the most notorious housing projects in Chicago. The Cabrini Green Projects were no joke and Karma had to walk by the sharks' everyday. Jay was actually from Cabrini Green which was where they initially met.

Karma grew up in a very dysfunctional environment with an absentee father figure and a very unconventional mom. Her mom's name was Leslie and she was also a Chicago native. Leslie always treated Karma as if her mere existence inconvenienced her. She repeatedly told Karma to be very careful of her actions because Karma could end up like her. Rest assured it was not out of concern it was strictly out of resentment. In Leslie's eyes Karma was a representation of her bad karma and she resented her daughter for that, hence the name.

Leslie instilled this negative attitude into Karma at a very young age. She was in fact the first person to break Karma's heart. Leslie would say and do such hurtful things to Karma. What made it worst was the fact that she was not high or drunk. She was 110% sober and the words she spoke were actually from her heart. Karma felt that her mother despised her and she honestly questioned if her mom had ever loved her.

Leslie's first and only priority was Leslie. She always made sure she had food, clothes and etc. Sometimes when Karma came home she would find empty food containers in the trash but not even scraps would be left for her. Karma was raised in poverty but her mom rarely yearned for anything. She never worked a day in her life but she always wore the finest threads and ate at the most expensive restaurants. Leslie was a prostitute and was not ashamed of it. For the right price she would do just about anything.

Leslie was not a complete dead beat so-to-speak because she did have somewhat of a conscience. On occasion she would give Karma these gifts that Karma referred to as guilt presents. Leslie's conscience never stopped her from doing anything but it haunted her like hell after.

Leslie and Karma lived in a downstairs two bedroom duplex. Leslie slept in one bedroom and the other bedroom was used as her closet. Karma did not even have a bedroom she slept on the living room couch.

When Karma was thirteen years old Leslie woke her up in the middle of the night. Leslie's boy toy of the hour was asleep in her bedroom but there was someone else at the door. His name was Mitchell but everyone knew him as Rich Mitch. He was Leslie's main john because he paid all of the bills, rent and utilities. His only condition was whenever he wanted some pussy she had to comply.

Rich Mitch did not care if Leslie fucked with other men just as long as he got his. It was about 1 o'clock in the morning when Leslie forced Karma to sit outside while she "entertained" Rich Mitch. Karma sat outside on the stairs in the middle of February by herself for two and half hours. The next day Leslie bought Karma a new outfit and a diamond tennis bracelet. Karma continued to accept her guilt presents until she learned that game recognized game.

The tables did a complete 360 once Karma turned sixteen. One night while Karma was walking home from Angel's house Rich Mitch pulled up next to her. He was driving a black Suburban on twenty-eight inch rims with dark tinted windows. Karma knew it was Rich Mitch because the initials RM were placed next to the Chevrolet emblem. Rich Mitch was definitely the H.N.I.C in their hood. He rolled down his passenger window.

Peering from the driver seat he said, "Get in little mama?"

"No that's ok I only have a little ways to go." Karma stated.

"I didn't ask you now hurry up and get in I got things to do" he said slightly irritated.

Not wanting to piss him off Karma walked over and climbed inside. The smell of weed and cherries lingered throughout the truck. Rich Mitch was dressed in a black Gucci jogging suit with a crisp white t-shirt underneath. He was wearing a necklace with a diamond medallion with the letters RM. In each of his ears he wore two of the biggest diamonds Karma had ever seen. She was trying not to stare but she had never seen him this up-close. Leslie always made certain that Karma was never alone nor to close with any of her men.

"Why you out so late" Rich Mitch asked.

"I was going to spend the night over my best friend's house but her boyfriend came over. I decided to walk home because I didn't want to be the third wheel." Karma said still amazed by how fine he was.

"You don't have a boyfriend?" he asked looking directly into her eyes.

"Umm no," she said somewhat embarrassed.

"I can't believe a girl as beautiful as you don't have a boyfriend. Real talk have you ever had a boyfriend?" he asked as they pulled into the McDonalds parking lot.

"I've never had a boyfriend. The boys at school don't like me because of the way I dress and my mom doesn't work so I don't have many options." Karma informed.

"Your mom means well shorty. Look I don't like seeing no one fucked up so I can throw you some change every now and then. You know for some gear and spending money," he offered as he began rolling a blunt while they sat in the McDonald's parking lot.

"For real" Karma excitedly questioned.

"Yeah fo'sho but you know nothing is free?" he said before lighting the blunt he had just rolled.

"My mom always says that but what would you need from me?" Karma asked sarcastically.

"Shorty, I don't need shit from you but there are a few things you could do for me," he said while inhaling the weed deeply.

"Like what?" Karma questioned.

At that moment Rich Mitch put the blunt he had been smoking into the ashtray. He then reached into his pants and pulled his dick out. Karma just stared at it because it was wide, long and dark like a cucumber. He began to stroke it gently and by doing so it began to grow bigger. Karma suddenly became scared because this was her first time seeing a dick in person. Especially a dick so big then all of sudden panic rushed her thoughts wondering what was he going to do to her.

"Ma why you looking all scared? You ain't ever seen a dick before? It ain't nothing to be scared of look come here and kiss it I promise it won't bite," he assured as he began stroking it again.

Karma leaned over the console and kissed the tip of his dick. He kept stroking it so she kissed it again. Rich Mitch's dick kept growing bigger and bigger. Karma had heard about girls giving head but she had never done it herself.

"Just keep kissing it," he said still stroking his dick.

Suddenly Rich Mitch began rubbing Karma's left breast forcing her nipple to peak through her shirt. Between her legs was pulsating and it began to feel slightly wet down there. She began moving uncomfortably in her seat trying to make the pulsating stop.

Rich Mitch lifted Karma's head and stuck his finger into her mouth. Karma kept sucking it while he directed his finger toward his lap and her lips followed. Rich Mitch then replaced his finger with his dick. The moment Karma's lips covered the tip of his dick she heard him gasp.

She looked up to see him resting his head on the headrest. He then lifted her shirt and began squeezing and pinching her nipples. His hands were causing a fire between Karma's legs so she began hungrily sucking his dick. She could not understand but the more and more he moaned and groaned the deeper she tried to go.

Rich Mitch hand suddenly moved down to her waist where he then unbuttoned her jeans. He began rubbing her pussy slowly. By now her head was bobbing out of control. Rich Mitch had one hand between her legs and then he inserted two fingers into her drenching wet pussy.

"Damn shorty you gon make me catch a case. Shit you got a nigga wanting to fill that pussy up," he whispered.

Karma did not bother responding she just kept sucking hoping that his fingers would not stop.

"Ah shit shorty I'm bout to cum catch it for me," he said while pounding her head into his dick.

Suddenly a thick liquid filled Karma's mouth that tasted weird and very salty.

"Shorty did you swallow?" he inquired with his hands still between her legs.

Karma held her breath and swallowed the nasty thick substance. After she swallowed she opened her mouth for his approval. Rich Mitch told her good job and pulled his hands from her pants and licked each of his fingers. They both buttoned their pants as Rich Mitch drove out of the parking lot. Karma did not know where he was taking her until they passed the Cabrini Green projects. He then pulled into her driveway without saying a word and let her out.

Karma felt different climbing out of his truck than she had felt climbing into it.

Surprisingly as Karma walked into the house she was greeted by her mother who was sitting on the couch. She must have been waiting on one of her men Karma thought as she walked past her mother toward the kitchen.

"Karma, I thought you were staying at Angel's house tonight." Leslie questioned.

"Yeah I was going to but I changed my mind is that ok?" Karma asked rhetorically.

"Whatever Karma don't pop no attitude with me cuz you ain't got no friends." Leslie said as she turned off the television.

"Karma you can come back in here I'm going to my room. Let me know when Rich Mitch gets here," she said as she closed her bedroom door.

Finally Karma thought as she grabbed her things and went back into the living room. She tried to call Angel but there was no answer. Karma waited and called a few more times but she finally gave up and began getting ready for bed. She took a long, hot shower but Karma still could not get Rich Mitch out of her mind. As she stepped out of the shower she wrapped a towel around her drenched hair and slipped on her robe. Karma brushed her teeth at least three times trying to get that nasty taste out of her mouth.

As Karma opened the bathroom door she caught her mother running toward the front door. Karma stared through the crack of the door as Rich Mitch kissed and hugged her mom. She watched as they walked towards her mother's room and closed the door.

As Karma sat on the couch she began applying coco butter to her legs. Thoughts of Rich Mitch rushed her mind as one of her hands drifted between her legs. She began slowly rubbing the area in circular motions. Her hand was feeling so good that she stretched her legs wider and sat back comfortably on the couch. Her pace began to quicken as she began grinding her hips on to her hand. Karma's body was on fire it felt like she was going to explode. Karma closed her eyes as she let one finger slip inside. She then slipped another finger in while still rubbing her pussy.

Karma opened her eyes to find Rich Mitch staring back at her. He stared at her for awhile before going into the bathroom. Karma was so embarrassed she did not know what to do. She ran into the kitchen to avoid the next awkward moment between them. Once she heard the bedroom door close she went back to the living room. Karma put on her t-shirt and went to sleep trying to forget what had just happened.

While Karma was sleeping she began feeling that same fire between her legs. Karma opened her eyes to find Rich Mitch on the end of the couch playing with her pussy. He began stroking that big cucumber and it began growing again. His fingers were feeling so good Karma's panties were drenched. Rich Mitch pulled her panties off and threw her blanket on to the floor.

Then suddenly his fingers stopped and Karma assumed he was going to make her suck his dick again. But instead he lowered his head between her legs and began feasting on her. Karma was trying to be quiet but it was feeling so good. Rich Mitch had her legs pushed back touching her ears. Karma could no longer control her moans as they got louder and louder. Rich Mitch made her bite on to a pillow as he kept licking. Without moving his tongue he stuck two fingers deep inside forcing a river of juices to depart from her body.

Karma felt physically spent but she still wanted to satisfy him. She slowly sat up from the couch and kneeled down between his legs. As he lay back on the couch her mouth covered his dick. Karma assumed that she was doing a good job by the way he kept banging her head. Then he suddenly stopped and pulled her up by her arms. Neither of them said a word and Karma immediately climbed onto his dick. He slowly inserted his dick inside of her with no condom. It hurt like hell at first but after it was in Karma did not want it to come out.

"Yea just like that," he whispered into her ear.

"Ahh yeah," Karma moaned.

"Turn around and bend over for daddy," Rich Mitch directed.

Karma did as she was told with juices still running from her legs. Rich Mitch then rammed his big dick inside of Karma. She was now biting the couch trying to stop her from screaming. He kept humping Karma as he pulled her by her hair forcing more juices to run.

"Ahh shit I'm I I'm coming," he stuttered.

Karma went to turn around to catch it but before she could he rammed his dick so far into her pussy she could not move. He continued to ram his dick inside of her until he came inside of Karma. His dick sent Karma into an instant coma.

When she awakened the next day she found three rubber band stacks of money inside of her book bag. Ironically, that was the first and last time Rich Mitch and Karma ever had sex. He still came to see Leslie but him and Karma never spoke to one another again. That was until she found out she was pregnant.

Karma knew the consequences of having unprotected sex but she did not think she would get pregnant on the first time. Karma swore that it should be something in the rule books against that. She knew she could not keep the baby nor could she tell her mom. Not sure of what to do Karma's fingers automatically dialed Angel. After about four rings she finally answered.

"Girl you ain't gon believe this shit," Karma said in a panic.

"Hi to you too," Angel said sarcastically.

"Angel fucks all the formalities I'm pregnant" Karma screamed.

"Ahh shit it's not Rich Mitch is it?" Angel asked already knowing the answer.

"Of course it is I've never slept with no one else"

"Damn Karma I thought yall used a rubber."

"Well it didn't work" Karma lied.

"Well you got to tell him maybe he'll pay for an abortion. Just tell him Karma." Angel said sympathetically.

"Angel what if my Mom finds out? She would kill me for real if she knew Rich Mitch was the father."

"Girl she won't find out call Rich Mitch and see what he says. If he front on you then we'll just put our heads together and come up with something." Angel assured.

"Thanks Angel I'm gonna call him right now. I'll call you right back." Karma said before hanging up.

Rich Mitch surprisingly did not deny the baby nor was he mad. He told Karma that she was too young to be having a baby. He also revealed to her that he was about to do some time. It turns out one of his soldiers had gotten arrested and was singing like a bird. He said he had taken a plea of three years which was a bargain but it was still three years.

Rich Mitch agreed to pay for the abortion and even offered to help Karma find her own place. Rich Mitch turned out to be a good guy. As a man of his word he took Karma to the clinic, bought her a house in River North and gave her a few grand to live on.

The day Karma moved was the last day she saw or spoke to her mother. Leslie ran off with one of her boy toys and never looked back. Angel moved in with Karma and they have been inseparable ever since.

Showtime

Angel pulled up to Karma's house and immediately prepared herself to hear Karma's mouth since it was twenty minutes after ten. Before she could open the car door she saw Karma rushing out. She had on a cute white Juicy Couture sweat suit with her favorite Coach flip flops. Karma was always fly but never over the top. Angel and Karma always said if you have to try too hard then you must not have it.

"It's about fucking time! Angel you ain't never on time. I should've woke yo ass up at like six this morning to get you here by nine." Karma said as she climbed into the truck.

"You know I had to get the kids together shit you try getting them together day in and day out.

They're either yelling at each other or telling on each other. Mommy this Mommy that Mommy is tired I need a vacation ASAP." Angel said while driving down Main Street.

"Girl I know but I'm just saying I called you three hours ago and you live five minutes from here. I know it's hard I'm just nervous about tonight." Karma said as she lit the blunt that she just removed from her Chanel purse.

"Damn girl you a weed head you haven't been in the truck five minutes and you already blazing up." Angel said as she got on the freeway.

"Whatever you know you gon hit this!" Karma said as she deeply inhaled the weed smoke.

"And you know this man!" Angel said doing her best impression of Chris Tucker in the movie Friday.

The two friends finished smoking their blunt and made there way into their favorite store Nordstrom's. They shopped and shopped but Karma still could not find an outfit for the night. Angel ended up buying a couple outfits and like three pairs of shoes. Karma and Angel had a serious shoe addiction. They probably owned over 500 shoes between the both of them. Of course Angel bought her kids a few outfits with the shoes to match. For every one thing she bought herself she always bought two things for her children.

Angel loved to shop but she was not one of those chicks that went shopping with every nickel they had. Angel was actually far from it damn near the opposite. Her husband DeMarcus paid for their house in cash so she did not have to worry about a mortgage. She had four vehicles; a white Denali, a green Range Rover and two old schools that were all paid for. Angel used her husband's stash and insurance money very wisely. She invested in real estate and opened a few small businesses. She owned a hair supply store in North River and a car wash on the Southside.

Angel complained sometimes but for the most part her life was great. She owed her lavish lifestyle to DeMarcus who had some illegal doings but was a very smart man. He had a pretty nice stash tucked away which is why she did not have to work a regular nine to five. Following DeMarcus's death Angel had become very depressed. She did not leave the house for almost two months. Meaning her and the kids did not have hardly any food. There were turn off notices and piles and piles of past due bills.

The kids were basically taking care of themselves. She had a wide awakening when she witnessed her children eating plain slices of white bread. At that moment she realized that she was taking her anger, pain and sorrow out on them. They did not deserve that and DeMarcus would have killed her if he was still alive. She promised from that day to never abandon them again be it physically or emotionally.

"Girl, it's already twelve lets got to Sak's real quick." Karma said trying to grip all of her bags.

"Alright, well hurry up because Madison's appointment is at 1:30 and I still have to pick her up." Angel said slightly flustered.

There were at least fifteen bags between the two of them. Why Karma did not have an outfit was unbeknown to Angel. They hurriedly rushed to the car and made their way to Sak's Fifth Avenue. As they walked into the door but before it closed Karma ran over to the clothing rack where a cute black dress was hanging.

"This is the one Angel, this is it." Karma said excitedly.

"It's cute but I know we didn't go through all of this for a little black dress. Karma for real you have like a million black dresses." Angel said.

"Whatever I don't have this dress." Karma said as she rummaged through the racks for her size.

After Karma purchased her little black dress Angel dropped her off at her house and went to pickup Madison from daycare. She had planned to drop Madison back off at daycare after her appointment. But she decided to pick them both up and make it a family day.

Jay had only one hour until show time and he still had a ton of things to do. Most importantly he still needed to pick up the ring he had specially made for Karma. Jay's thoughts were frazzled he had so many things to do and not too much time left. He still needed to get dressed but he could not seem to think straight.

Man up is what he kept repeating to himself but his nerves were getting the best of him. He wanted tonight to be perfect. Karma was the only woman to bring out that soft side of him. He was usually calm and laid back but here he was pacing the floor like a bitch he thought. Finally he grabbed his car keys off of the counter and jumped into his ebony black Tahoe. He drove until he arrived at Tam's Custom Jewelry. He was considered a preferred shopper because he purchased all of his jewelry from Tam's. As he walked into the store he noticed Isaac the owner approaching him with what appeared to be a ring box.

"What's up man?" Jay said walking into his direction.

"You, I thought you may have gotten cold feet." Isaac said with a slight grin.

"Man I den came this far I might as well cross the finish line, you know." Jay said.

"Well here it is." Isaac said as he extended his hand with a now open ring box.

"Damn man this shit right here is what it do. Man how much we talking about cuz this shit right here look like it's worth some serious stacks." Jay said still amazed.

"Man that right there is a gift from me to you. You've been a loyal customer since day one. I want you to really give my offer some thought." Isaac said.

"Yo, I can't take this you've done enough for me."

"You remind me of myself growing up and I wish I had someone to steer me in the right direction. You are very smart Jay and if you serious about marrying that girl then you need a plan. You can't raise no family on drug money and you better not involve that girl in all your illegal wrong doings. If you serious then you better man up" Isaac said seriously.

"Man I hear you I'm gonna really think about it but man here's five stacks in the meantime." Jay said as he handed him five rubber band stacks of money.

"Nope I want you to hold that five stacks and think about what we discussed. When you decide then that's when we'll negotiate a price." Isaac said pushing Jay's hand away.

"Man you know what I really respect you and no one has ever tried so hard to get me out dis game. It's really hard to trust people especially after what happened with that old head Slim. I would have never suspected him to be an informant. Maybe that was a blessing in disguise cuz if he didn't kill his self I would have. Man you know what you're right about Karma I can't bring her into this world. I'm going to accept your offer but I still have a couple loose ends to tie up but after that I'm out." Jay sincerely said.

"That's what I'm talking about I know that fast money is nice but I'm offering you a partnership in a multi-million dollar company. Man don't think living right ain't fine living because you won't see me in a Honda. Man I rides nothing but the best, American made Cadillac's." Isaac said proudly.

"Man I know but the streets are my comfort zone. I am ready to change though. I mean since I got the opportunity to change I better take it while I can before the man chooses for me. You know what you alright with me Isaac you alright with me. I'm gon holla at you later man." Jay said as they hugged and shook hands.

As Jay hoped into his truck he reflected on his life and how it was about to change. As a little boy he had always dreamed of being a trap star. Look at him now trading in his trap star status for a family. Not really though because once a G always a G. He paid the streets twenty-eight years of his life. He started this shit when he was about thirteen years old. But the streets had been scouting him long before then.

Ironically, his father was apart of his life and he surprisingly did take care of him. Unfortunately, he was murdered by Jay's uncle when Jay was only nine years old. Jay used to believe that was where his bitterness stemmed from. On that day he lost his dad and his uncle the only male figures he had known.

Jay's mom Loretta was a "g" in her heart. After his dad was murdered the police claimed to have no leads in the case. Loretta decided to take matters into her own hands. The streets were already talking that Jay's uncle was the culprit behind the murder. Loretta ultimately paid some stick-up boys to take him out which they did and Jay never saw him again.

If only Jay's imagination was reality then that story would demonstrate an inch of truth. The reality was Jay's dad was a bitch and his mom was addicted to heroin. He had not seen either of them since he was about sixteen years old. His so called mother played him and sold him out to get high. Jay trusted her which is probably why he never really trusted women. Real talk he blamed her for his little brother Shaun's death too. Jay did indeed avenge his brother's death but he was not the cause of it.

Jay believed if Loretta would have been there then Shaun would still be alive. Jay tried to be there but he could not or just did not but either way Shaun was no longer there. Reflecting back on his life made Jay more certain about marrying Karma. Jay became instantly excited again about marrying her. His nerves seem to ease some as his heart reassured his mind that Karma was the one.

Breathe Karma breathe is what she kept repeating to herself. Her hair was pulled back into an elegant bun and the edges were precisely smoothed into place. The short black dress she had purchased earlier fit her body like a glove. It was not raunchy or video hoe like it was Marilyn Monroe sexy. Even though she turned out to be a hoe we all know the classic look Karma was channeling. Karma accessorized with a single diamond necklace, dainty diamond studs and a diamond tennis bracelet. She completed her look with black Gucci pumps and the matching Gucci purse. Her makeup was flawless down to her eyelashes while her lips were painted a subtle yet ravishing red.

Karma was excited but she was still nervous as hell. She decided to walk over to the bar in the living room and poured herself a shot of Patron. She completely downed the shot of Patron and her nerves began to slightly loosen up. Suddenly the doorbell rang and the butterflies inside of her stomach returned. She quickly poured herself another shot of Patron and downed it as well. She glanced at the bottle of Patron contemplating another shot but she decided against it. Karma walked through the living room to the front door. She took a deep breath then answered.

"Angel what are you doing here?" Karma asked.

"Girl this is an emergency bathroom stop." Angel said as Madison burst through the door running toward the bathroom.

"Girl Jay is gonna be here any minute." Karma said as Angel and Mason walked inside.

"I know I'm sorry but she had to go really bad and honestly I thought you guys would have already left by now." Angel said as Madison peeked around the corner.

"I'm sorry Auntie Kar I couldn't hold it." Madison said in the most innocent voice Karma had ever heard.

Those boys better watch out when she gets older she is going to be something else. Karma thought silently.

"It's ok you know auntie house is always open for you." Karma said as she zipped up Madison's jacket.

After Mason went to the bathroom Angel gathered her children and left. Karma locked the door behind them then turned around and rested her head against the door. Jay was going to be here any minute Karma thought as panic began to resurface. She closed her eyes in search of some tranquility or at least sanity because she was completely losing it. Her thoughts were suddenly interrupted by the sound of the doorbell which startled her somewhat. Karma turned around and closed her eyes with her hand on the door knob she silently counted to ten. She then proceeded to open the door.

"Oh my God Karma you look beautiful!" Jay said in awe.

Jay was fine and tonight he was definitely giving Morris Chestnut and Denzel Washington a run for their money. He was dressed in a perfectly tailored Armani suit with a grey satin shirt underneath. He topped it off with a grey and black stripped tie. On his neck rested a diamond encrusted necklace with a cross pendant and his ears were laced with the largest diamonds Karma had ever seen. On his wrist was a black and platinum Audemar's Piguet watch with the matching platinum cufflinks. His hair was his usual low cut fade with 360 degree waves that were as deep as the Atlantic. Karma was so marveled by Jay's appearance she did not even notice the two dozen long stem roses he was carrying.

"Thank you! You look pretty handsome yourself." Karma said as she opened the door further to give him a hug and a peck on his cheek.

Before Karma could kiss his check he quickly turned his head forcing their lips to meet. They kissed for what seemed like eternity for the first time. Sure they had messed around a couple of times in the past but they were never really affectionate toward one another.

"Damn baby what has gotten into you?" Karma said trying to catch her breath.

"I haven't got into you yet." he said mischievously.

"You are such a mess." Karma said playfully pushing him before allowing him to come inside.

"Sorry I'm late but we gotta hurry up we got an eight o' clock reservation at Charlie Trotter's." Jay said as he picked up Karma's jacket from the coat rack.

"Ok, Ok let me turn off all of the lights." Karma said as she hit the light switch.

Karma walked back over to the hallway where Jay was standing holding her jacket. He held her coat as she slipped into it and they made their way to the truck. Jay opened her door and assisted her inside of the truck like a perfect gentleman.

There were still some butterflies inside of Karma's stomach but the Patron definitely helped. As Jay drove on the Circle interchange Scarface's "Never" blasted from the speakers. Jay pulled up to the valet in front of Charlie Trotters and the valet attendant proceeded to escort Karma out of the truck. She waited on the curb for Jay as he exited the car and grabbed the ticket from the attendant.

"Come on you ready?" Jay asked as he extended his arm to Karma.

"Yes," she said locking arms with him.

As they entered the restaurant ignorance attempted to take away from their shine but Jay was not having it.

"Excuse me this restaurant is by reservation only and we're booked but there's an array of other restaurants along the strip." the host smugly said.

"Despite the array of other restaurants I have a reservation here. The name is Jay Stevenson and will you let Michael know that I would like a word with him." Jay calmly said.

"Oh, Mr. Stevenson um Mr. Gold go Goldberg has been expecting you I I I apologize for the um mix up." the host stuttered.

"Can we be seated?" Jay said no longer acknowledging the host.

"Yes yes of course sir right this way." the host said as he scurried ahead of them.

"They all the same they assume a black man is lost when he's out of the hood. But money talks everywhere!" Jay whispered to Karma.

After they were seated Jay ordered a bottle of Ace of Spades. They sipped their champagne as they absorbed the beautiful view in front of them. As they waited for their food to arrive Jay and Karma conversed about their favorite pastime, sports. It may not sound romantic but this was hands down the best date either of them had been on. After they left the restaurant they got into the truck but Jay became suspiciously quiet.

"So where are we going now." Karma asked

"It's a surprise just sit back we'll be there in a little while." Jay said as he rubbed her thigh.

And just that quick between Karma's legs became warm and slightly sticky. To calm her nerves she decided to pour herself another glass of Ace of Spades from the bar in the back seat. Upon finishing her glass of champagne she noticed they were nearing the airport. As they pulled into the parking lot Jay drove through but he did not stop. He went through another gate that led them to an unaccompanied plane.

"Oh my God Jay is you serious? Jay we ain't getting on that plane! Oh my God Jay" Karma said unable to hide her excitement.

"Yes we are and I hope you don't get air sick because we're gonna be up there for awhile." Jay said as he turned off the car ignition.

"Oh my God Jay I'm speechless! No one has ever done anything like this for me." Karma said as she reached over the console to hug him.

As they hugged something changed in the universe and their lips met for the second time this evening. But this time they kissed for what seemed like hours as Jay caressed her body softly. Karma felt as if she was under a trance because she wanted to literally taste all of him. When they finally came for up air they were both taken aback by the connection. But before either one of them could speak an older white man knocked on the window.

Jay rolled the window down and the courteous gentleman introduced himself as Captain Bob. He then informed them everything was a go and they could aboard the plane. After boarding the plane the two lovebirds had gotten comfortable. They drank, laughed and watched movies until Karma passed out.

Karma was awakened by Captain Bob speaking but she only heard the tail end of the conversation. She immediately sat up and opened her eyes to make sure she heard him correctly. Did he just say that we just arrived in Las Vegas? No it could not be or could it?

"Jay wake up." Karma said as she pushed him slowly.

"Jay wake up are we in Las Vegas?" she asked again still pushing him.

"Yeah" Jay mumbled before kissing her.

Karma could not believe she was in Las Vegas. She was so excited and could not wait to tell Angel. Jay had to be the only man who rents a jet and takes a woman across the country for a date Karma thought. As the plane came to a halt Captain Bob informed the two they were able to exit the plane.

It was just a little after midnight once they arrived in Las Vegas. Karma wanted to go to the room and freshen up but jay insisted that they tour the hotel. It was a perfect night as they strolled outside the casino. The next door they walked through appeared to be the doorway to heaven. As they walked through Karma admired the beautiful pool and climbed on the edge. She ran her fingers through the waterfall but when she turned around Jay was on one knee. He grabbed her hand and the tears began to fall.

"Karma I love you! You are my first and last. There is nothing that I would not do for you! I want to spend the rest of my life trying to give you the world. Karma will you marry me?" Jay asked as a single tear fell from his eye.

"Yes! Yes Jay I'll marry you!" Karma said as she jumped into his arms.

At that moment Karma realized that sometimes it may seem like God is throwing you lemons but in the end he is always on time. After Jay proposed it was a little after midnight they decided to gamble for awhile before going to bed. The couple decided to sleep in separate suites until their wedding night.

Once Karma made it back to her room she immediately called Angel. It did not dawn onto her the time difference until she looked at clock on the nightstand. Overcome with excitement Karma continued dialing and the phone rang three times before a not so happy Angel answered.

"What, this better be life or death!" Angel said.

"Oh my god Angel Jay proposed!" Karma screamed.

"Congratulations he told me about it earlier." Angel said trying to wake up.

"What! You knew why didn't you give me a heads up? I'm in Vegas with no extra clothing or shoes nothing just the clothes on my back." Karma questioned.

"He wanted to surprise you if I would've said something it would have ruined it. Forget what you're talking bout cuz everything you named is material. I mean come on Karma you are in Vegas I'm sure you can buy an outfit."

"Yeah you're right I'm trippin I'm just so excited. I wish you were here."

"Yeah but I'm really happy for you! You know I love you but its four in the morning can you call me back when the sun comes up."

"Oh, I'm so sorry Angel I forgot. Jay said the wedding is going to be tomorrow. We're going to have another one in Chicago when we get back. So I'll see you when we return as Mr. and Mrs. Stevenson. Ahhhh! I'm so excited." Karma uttered.

"Alright girl I'm excited too and you better not play me on my dress." Angel said before hanging up.

A few hours later Karma went shopping for the perfect wedding dress and found it. It was a Vera Wang original that precisely fit her slim yet curvy figure. She decided against wearing white because her conscience would not allow her to. She chose a long, sleeveless, ivory dress with a plunging neckline. Not like the infamous J-Lo dress but just enough to show Jay he had chosen the right woman. There were also a thin flow of flowers over her right shoulder. She borrowed jewelry from Harry Winston to add the finishing touches to her glamorous look.

The ceremony was beautiful it was not cheesy like those drive-thru weddings. It was actually held in the Garden of Gods Pool Oasis which is the same place where he had proposed. When Karma walked into the Versailles inspired gazebo at a quarter to midnight she almost passed out. It was very beautiful and Jay looked extremely handsome in his tuxedo. The two recited their own vows and kissed one another as they were now Mr. and Mrs. Stevenson. Jay and Karma spent the rest of the week in Vegas rarely leaving their honeymoon suite.

The newlyweds made their way back to Chicago only to find out they were moving to New Jersey. Jay had gone into business with a jeweler named Isaac who owned Tam's Custom Jewelry. Isaac was actually expanding his business and he wanted Jay to oversee the New Jersey location. With the grand opening in less than a month Jay and Karma canceled their Chicago wedding plans. They felt they could never outdo their initial wedding and opted to focus on moving.

Haters & Cheaters

Karma gazed out of the kitchen window just before preparing breakfast. Unbeknown to her someone was observing her every move. That someone was a blast from her past which Karma thought she had left behind in Chicago. Asia Buchanan was back in full effect and was ready to end Karma's so called fairytale. Asia believed the lavish life Karma now lived should have been hers.

Jay loved Asia but it did not match his love for Karma. Asia knew that as well but all she could see was the glitz and the glam. She resented the fact that Jay and Karma resided in a luxury condominium in Hamilton, New Jersey. While Karma was busy driving a Range Rover Asia did not even own a car. Asia left

Chicago in hopes to win Jay's heart back. She had not seen Jay since their last encounter and had no idea of his whereabouts. Until one day while Asia was watching a popular rapper named J-Rock's reality show. She watched on as J-Rock visited his favorite jeweler, Tam's Custom Jewelry. Her prayers were then answered as J-Rock approached the owner who appeared to be Jay. Asia could not believe her eyes and at that moment the search begun.

Asia had been tracking Karma's every move since she arrived in New Jersey via the Greyhound bus. It was now going on two months and Asia still had no plan of attack. The more she observed Jay and Karma the madder she became because their life appeared to be perfect. Contrary to Asia's beliefs things were not as peachy as they seemed in the Stevenson household.

Jay and Karma had been living in New Jersey as man and wife for over a year. Some say after the first year of marriage the newness ware's off. Well the honeymoon was definitely over because they had become your typical married couple. Karma was unhappy but she could not deny that Jay was a great husband. He was a great provider and was neither controlling nor demanding. Karma did not have a want in the world. She did not have to wake up at a certain time nor did she have to cook daily.

Everyday Karma woke up at the same time and cooked the same breakfast. Over the course of a year the two had literally became robots. Jay would drink his usual orange juice with a side of water while Karma preferred milk. During breakfast Jay would read the sports section of the paper while Karma read the Arts and Life section. Their sex life was regular but it was always planned in advance.

The only time Karma experienced any type of spontaneity was at her boutique called Down Bottom located in Manhattan, New York. Down Bottom was an upscale boutique specializing in couture and urban wear. It had been open for seven months and business was doing pretty good for New York. If they were located somewhere in Ohio their profits would be considered booming. The overhead cost for a commercial lot in Manhattan was absolutely ridiculous.

On the other hand Jay's jewelry store was doing very big things. Tam's Custom Jewelry was located in Connecticut. It was a joint venture with Jay's friend, Isaac who also owned a jewelry store in Chicago.

Initially Isaac wanted Jay to manage one of his stores but Jay was better fit as a partner. His transition from street hustler to diamond designer was remarkable. He catered to more celebrities then regular folk so-to-speak. A few rappers even shouted him out in a couple of their songs. From the outside looking in everything appeared to be perfect but looks can definitely be deceiving.

Today Karma planned to put the spark back into her marriage. First she went to pick up some new toys for them to play with. Her next stop was Victoria's Secret where she found something that was sure to get his attention. Karma rushed home, took a shower and got dressed. She wanted to get to the store after his employees had left but before Jay left.

Karma arrived a little after nine o'clock to be sure that he was alone.

As she pulled up she observed two of his employees leaving. Karma opened her door to exit but stopped when a woman walked up to the store's door. Karma thought it was probably just a customer until she went into her purse and pulled out a key. She proceeded to unlock the door and walked inside. Karma felt like a complete fool but maybe the unfamiliar woman was just a friend. She knew she was reaching because what kind of friend would have a key to her husbands' business and Karma had never met them.

Suddenly it dawned on Karma that Jay was having an affair. She waited for awhile before using her own key to follow the unfamiliar woman inside.

An unaccompanied Jay was sitting at his desk studying orders and inventory. Deep in thought the sound of a woman's voice broke his concentration.

He looked up and saw Cheryl leaning against the door.

"Hey baby." Jay said as Cheryl walked through the door.

"Baby I've been missing you all day." Cheryl said as she climbed on top of his desk.

"Damn baby I've been missing you too but I have to take care of this and then I will take care of you." Jay said as he kissed her lips.

"You may get away with that with your wife but you won't with me." Cheryl said as she dropped to her knees.

Cheryl then unbuckled his pants as he sat back and rested his head on the headrest. She proceeded to pull his dick out of his pants and began gently massaging it. As she massaged it she began leaving soft kisses on the head and finally she covered him with her mouth.

"You want me to stop?" she mumbled.

Jay did not even respond he just grabbed her head and held it in place as she slurped his dick.

"Am I better then her?" she retorted with his dick still inside of her mouth.

Before Jay could respond Cheryl stuffed his dick and balls into her mouth. He could no longer hold it as he pulled out and squirted all over her face. Jay pulled her up and threw her on top of the desk without even wiping her face off. He then grabbed a condom from his desk drawer and proceeded to fuck the shit out of her.

"Ah fuck I'm about to come." Jay said as he rammed his dick deep inside of her filling the condom.

"Why don't you ever eat my pussy?" Cheryl asked as she fixed her dress.

"I don't eat pussy." Jay said nonchalantly.

"You probably eat her pussy."

"And if I did she's my wife." Jay said becoming slightly irritated.

"Are you ever going to leave her?" Cheryl asked.

"No!"

"So why are you fucking me?" Cheryl screamed.

"Because I can but ain't nobody forcing you to do shit. As a matter of fact let's end this because you're too attached."

"You know what fuck you Jay." Cheryl said as she stormed out. After reaching the door she turned and said.

"You haven't seen the last of me because karma's a bitch." she said as she slammed the door.

Jay continued working as if the entire situation with Cheryl had not occurred. After finishing his work he locked the store up and drove home. Jay was eager to see Karma but what he did not know was that Karma had just seen everything.

Karma had actually left a couple of minutes before Cheryl. She could not believe she had just watched and recorded her husband fucking someone else. Karma was completely heart-broken. She sincerely believed Jay loved her but maybe she was the only one living a fairytale. Tears rolled down Karma's face uncontrollably as she drove. She did not have a particular destination but she needed to getaway.

Karma could not go home because she was not ready to face Jay yet. She then wondered if Jay would have tried to fuck her that night. The thought alone just disgusted her. Trying to erase the picture out of her head Karma reached into the console and found her Mary J CD. Karma knew if anything could get her through this Mary was a sure win. As Share My World blasted through the speakers Karma lit a freshly rolled blunt and just drove.

Karma continued to drive as well as ignore all 117 missed calls from Jay. She finally took a break and decided to pull into a rest stop. Karma put the car in park as her phone began ringing for the umpteenth time. She decided it was time to finally face Jay and just answer. Karma picked up the phone and surprisingly it read Angel in the caller id.

"Hello!"

"Bitch don't hello me I've been blowing up your phone all night. Jay called me all panicked because you didn't come home. Karma what is wrong with you are you ok?" Angel screamed.

"No Angel, Jay is cheating on me!" Karma said as her voice began to crack.

"What do you mean how do you know?" Angel inquired.

"I went to surprise him and he was with her and they were. Angle I watched my husband fuck another woman." Karma said as she completely broke down on the phone.

"Oh my God Karma, It's gonna be ok did they see you? Do you know the bitch?" Angel inquired further.

"They didn't see me and I don't know her but she knows of me." Karma said as the tears continued to fall at a rapid pace.

"What do you mean?" Angel asked somewhat confused.

"The whole time they were fucking she kept saying shit like your wife can't do this or that. She kept asking if she was better and Jay wouldn't say nothing." Karma said wiping the tears from her face.

"I can't believe him I'm ready to go fuck both of them up!" Angel amply stated.

"I taped it Angel I don't know why but I taped it. I had brought the camera to tape me and Jay but he." Karma said unable to finish her sentence.

"Karma where are you I'm going to the airport right now!" Angel said.

"I'm not sure I think I'm close to PA but I'm not sure though." Karma said looking around the empty parking lot.

"Ok Karma I need you to go get a hotel. I'm on my way I'm going call my mom and see if she can come over so I don't have to wake the kids. Everything is going to be fine once you get to the hotel call and let me know where it is ok." Angel said in a concerned tone.

"Thank you Angel, I really don't know what I would do without you." Karma said wiping her tears away.

"Girl you my sister I love you and I know you would do the same for me in a heartbeat. So go get a room and I'll see you shortly." Angel said before hanging up.

I love you too Karma whispered as she sat her cell phone on the console. A million questions began to bombard Karma's mind. I thought we were happy I thought I was a good wife but I guess not Karma concluded. She had no idea what her next move was going to be she was torn between leaving Jay and staying with him. Karma thought about revenge but she ultimately decided against it.

She wondered how long Jay had been fucking that girl she hopelessly wanted to believe it was just a sex thing. Does he take her out I mean does everyone know that he has been playing me Karma questioned. She hated him but Karma still loved him even though she kept picturing herself killing him. Karma needed to calm down like Angel said so she began breaking down another shell. She then lit the freshly rolled blunt and pulled out of the rest area parking lot.

As Karma merged onto the freeway the tension in her body began to loosen as she inhaled the blunt. The more she puffed the more she felt like everything was going to be alright.

Karma exited the freeway and pulled into the parking lot of Motel 9. It was not the Ritz Carlton but Karma was really feeling those four blunts and the last thing she needed was to get pulled over in the middle of nowhere. Karma paid for the double bedroom and braced herself for the absolute worst as she opened the door. Surprisingly it was not that bad. Again it was not the Ritz but it was not the projects either.

Karma removed her jacket, turned on the television and walked toward the bathroom. She then turned on the shower and began to undress before entering the hot and steamy shower. Karma let the water just run off of her body for almost thirty minutes until she realized that she had forgot to call Angel. She quickly washed up and wrapped a towel around her body. Karma went back into the bedroom and searched through her purse for her cell phone. After retrieving it she dialed Angel's number.

"Hey my bad girl I was smoking on that Kush and completely forgot to call you." Karma explained while wrapping her wet hair up in a towel.

"Girl don't sweat it what hotel are you at?" Angel inquired.

"Motel 9 it's right off of I-80 in PA. I'm not far from the airport so I can pick you up when you land." Karma offered.

"Ok well its fifteen minutes before five and I'm on the freeway. The flight leaves at 5:45 this morning so I'll call you when I land." Angel hurriedly said.

"Oh ok be safe Angel you know how you drive." Karma said smiling for the first time that night.

"Whatever I'll see you in a few." Angel said before hanging up.

Karma grabbed the remote from the nightstand and began flipping through the channels. There was nothing on TV so she ended up drifting off to sleep. She was awakened by someone banging on the door. The sun was brightly shining through the cracks of the vertical blinds as her eyes peered opened. As she stood up she rewrapped the towel around her body.

Karma walked toward the door as the banging continued but she could now hear someone faintly calling her name. As she reached for the door she glanced in the peep hole to find a very frustrated Angel. Karma quickly unfastened the security lock and opened the door.

"Damn girl I've been calling and calling you. I even had housekeeping try to get in here but you had the security latch on." Angel said as she walked into the room.

"Oh my god Angel I'm so sorry. Girl after I got off of the phone with you it was lights out." Karma said.

"Its cool but I'm hungry as hell. I saw a Denny's down the street on the cab ride here." Angel said as she opened her suitcase. "Here I brought you some clothes go throw them on and lets roll." Angel said as she handed Karma a yellow Baby Phat sweat suit.

"Girl good looking I didn't want to walk in there in my trench coat and teddy." Karma said as she removed her towel and put on the sweat suit. She did not have any undergarments but it was a lot better than that trench coat.

When Angel finished rolling their pre-breakfast blunt they left. Karma and Angel puffed away as they drove to Denny's so much so that by the time they arrived the blunt was damn near gone. It was a little after ten and they now had a serious case of the munchies.

The two friends basically ordered the entire menu from pancakes to cheese fries. They did not leave Denny's until almost 1 o'clock. Surprisingly neither one of them even mentioned Jay. Of course they found a mall so they shopped until they were hungry again.

By the time they left the mall it was going on 8 o'clock. Shopping really wore them out so they decided to just pick up some Chinese food and head back to the hotel. Before they reached the room they passed a local liquor store. Needless to say they turned around and bought some Patron and Cuevo.

After arriving at the hotel Karma and Angel each took showers and sat down for dinner. After dinner the two traded multiple shots of Patron and Cuevo. They were now a little buzzed from the tequila so they did the most logical thing and rolled a blunt. As they lay across the bed the two friends smoked the kush and drank a few more shots. Angel stood up to go to the bathroom but ended up falling into Karma's lap. Angel burst out laughing as Karma's night gown strap fell exposing her right breast. Her nipple then began to harden as the cold air grazed it.

The two friends immediately stopped laughing as they both became motionless. As Angel lay across Karma's lap something awkward happened and she felt attracted to her. When Karma's nipple sprouted out Angel shockingly wanted to taste her and unbeknown to Angel Karma wanted her to. Angel reached for her but Karma pulled away.

Feeling rejected Angel rolled over on to her stomach not sure about what had just occurred. But then Karma climbed onto Angel's back and sat between her lower back and her ass. Karma slowly and gently began to massage Angel's back. Karma began kissing Angel on her neck as her bare breast rubbed against Angel's back. A slight moan escaped Angel's lips as Karma began to gyrate on top of her. The two friends were treading a fine line and entering unknown territory. Hormones were mounting causing Angel to begin gyrating as well. She then turned onto her back and Karma was completely unclothed. Karma pulled off her tank top and threw it to the floor.

Suddenly Angel said, "Karma stop we're both drunk and high let's just go to sleep."

Karma realized Angel was right and the two friends went to their separate beds. Both were hoping the other would not remember what had just happened.

The next morning Karma found herself replaying last night's events. She had been awake for almost an hour but was scared to open her eyes. She could not believe what had happened between her and Angel. Karma began to panic oh my god what have I done Angel is my best friend. What if Angel is really a lesbian Karma questioned? Oh no what if Angel thinks we are together now. Karma wished she could sleep through this nightmare. Another hour passed and she finally opened her eyes.

Karma turned to see where Angel was but the room was empty. As she sat on the edge of the bed her head began to throb. She picked up her cell phone from the end table. She knew Jay was at home going crazy but fuck him she thought. He should not have been out there cheating she concluded. She flipped her sidekick open and it read 59 missed calls. Wow she thought. At that moment she decided it was time to call Jay.

"Karma" Jay answered on the first ring.

"Yeah" Karma said nonchalantly.

"Are you ok? Where have you been? I've been calling you all night. I've been worried sick about you."

"Um Angel was," she began to say before he interrupted.

"I called Angel and she didn't know where the fuck you were. Are you cheating on me Karma?" Jay angrily questioned.

He had some nerve trying to check her Karma thought. Composure is what she kept repeating to herself.

"What the fuck Jay! Of course I'm not cheating on you. Angel called me all upset so I thought it would be nice to surprise her. I tried to call you but your phone was going straight to voicemail. I called you at work but you weren't in today. The house phone was busy all night. I was about to ask you were you cheating on me." Karma lied.

"Man whatever Karma where are you?" Jay hastily asked.

"I'm in PA but I'll be home in a couple of days." she assured.

"Yeah do that because we got a lot to talk about." Jay said as he hung up.

Who the fuck does he think he is Karma questioned. He hung up on her pissed but he was in fact the one having an affair. Karma proceeded to get up and take a shower. I fucking hate him she thought as she turned on the shower. Karma questioned if her life could get any worst as she stepped into the steamy shower. She let the water just trickle over her body as she inhaled the steam. Things always seemed so much clearer after she had taken a shower. The hot water began to cool so she turned off the shower and dried off. Karma grabbed the robe from the back of the door. She opened the door and walked over to the sink to brush her teeth. After doing so she turned around and was shocked to see Angel sitting on the bed.

"Girl you scared the shit out of me." Karma said still somewhat startled.

"My fault I just got back a couple of minutes ago."

"Oh where you go?"

"I needed some air last night was um unexpected to say the least. Honestly, I wasn't sure how to act because I've never done anything like that." Angel said.

"I know I was thinking the same thing lets just keep this between us. I mean we were drunk it's not like we're lesbians now." Karma assured.

"Yeah you're right we'll take this secret to our grave." Angel insured.

"Anyways I called Jay earlier?" Karma said as she threw on another jogging suit that Angel had brought her.

"Really what did he say?"

"Girl he was mad as hell anyways I told him I'll be home in a couple of days. I should surprise his ass and come back today." Karma pondered.

"Yeah but what are you gonna do are you going to stay with him or at least confront him." Angel asked.

"I don't know yet but karma's a bitch."

"Girl you're crazy let's go eat." Angel said as she walked toward the door.

"I know I'm crazy and he's about to find out." Karma said as they walked toward her truck.

The two ended up eating at this small neighborhood diner down the street. After eating Karma decided it was time to go home and face the music. They said their goodbyes and went in their separate directions. As Karma drove down the freeway she suddenly became nauseous. She immediately pulled over and proceeded to cough up her insides on the side of the road. Once there was nothing else to cough up she jumped back into the truck. What else could go wrong she thought as she merged back on to the road?

As Karma drove she reached into the middle console and pulled out a freshly rolled blunt. She inhaled it deeply and began to devise the ultimate plan of revenge.

Three's Company

Jay would have never suspected that Karma was cheating on him. He had his share of jump offs on the side but he did not love any of them. Jay loved the shit out of Karma and he would give her the world if he could. Even if she was cheating she did not even have the decency to come home. She just ups and leaves without calling, writing a note or at least sending a text message.

Jay had been worried as hell about her. He did not know what he was going to say to her when she decided to come home. The crazy part was that he had just run into Asia and he turned her down. He told her that he was happily married and he meant it. But now with Karma doing disappearing acts he did not know. Jay had always trusted Karma he never had a reason not to.

As he sat at the bar he heard the garage door open. Jay looked at his watch and it was fifteen minutes after seven. He had been praying to hear the sound of the garage door but now the sound annoyed him. It sent an instant rage throughout his body. His hands began to shake as his nostrils started to flare.

Before Jay knew it he was already half way down the stairs. He met Karma at the door and immediately threw her against the wall. His rage had taken over his body and he was no longer in control. Tears began to run down Karma's face as Jay repeatedly slammed her against the wall. He then drew his hand back but before he struck her he suddenly dropped his hand. What am I doing he thought as he slowly stepped away from her.

As Jay gazed into Karmal's eyes for the first time he saw fear. He looked down at his hands then back at Karma.

"Why Jay, what is wrong with you?" Karma said as tears heavily fell from her eyes.

"I I ahh I'm so sorry I I don't know what came over me." Jay stuttered as tears began to form in his eyes.

Karma did not respond she just slid to the floor and when she did her blood smeared down the wall as she fell. Jay attempted to pick her up but she forcefully pushed him away.

"Don't touch me Jay get away from me." Karma screamed.

Jay slowly backed away from Karma and he gradually walked upstairs. Jay sat at the top of stairs waiting for Karma to leave or doubtfully come upstairs. He wanted her to understand that he did not mean it. Honestly, how did she expect him to react to her leaving without calling? She had not been home for damn near two days and she just casually strolls in here Jay thought. Damn. She could really be hurt he thought as he stared at the blood stained wall. He rested his head on the wall by the stair rail. Before long he had fallen asleep wishing this was all a dream.

Jay finally opened his eyes to find Karma's body sprawled across the cement floor. Jay walked down the stairs and gently picked her up. He then carried her to their bedroom and laid her across the bed. He could not see if there was a knot but with the amount of blood that was on the wall he scheduled a doctor's appointment for her. At that point he did not know how she would feel or react to him so he called off work. If she was not ok he would have liked to have at least been there since he was the blame.

Jay decided to cook breakfast even though pancakes could not heal this situation they could not hurt. He then took a shower and threw on some sweats and a white t-shirt. Jay began preparing Karma's favorite pecan apple pancakes with bacon and eggs. After breakfast was complete he went downstairs and cleaned her blood from the wall. As he walked back toward the kitchen he found Karma looking at the stove. Jay had no clue of what to say and he assumed she did not either. Karma began fixing their plates and they ate breakfast with neither one of them saying a peep. As Jay picked up Karma's plate to put it in the sink Karma finally spoke.

"Jay you promised me. You had every right to be upset with me but to put your hands on me. Jay you said you would never lay your hands on me or any woman for that matter. After everything that happened with your mom how could you do this to me? I've never done anything for you to bash my head in." Karma innocently said as she stared deeply into his eyes.

"Karma I'm sorry I don't know what came over me but you know I love you. There's nothing in this world that I wouldn't do for you. Please Karma forgive me please don't leave me I need you." Jay said on bending knee with his head in Karma's lap.

Tears began to fall as Karma rubbed the back of Jay's head. Karma was dressed in a white robe that exposed her thighs. Jay began slowly kissing and caressing her outer thighs until a slight moan escaped her mouth. He then gently parted Karma's legs and continued to kiss her inner thighs. As he kissed he inserted one finger inside of her. As his finger went in and out of her she opened her legs further. Jay's tongue began to probe her insides as he inserted another finger. He gently licked and sucked on her click until she screamed and her juices filled his mouth.

Karma stood up, removed her robe and bent across the kitchen table. Taking the hint Jay dropped his sweat pants and inserted his dick inside of her from the back. Jay began with slow strokes but eventually quickened his pace.

"I'm sorry baby." Jay said as he pushed deep inside of her.

"Ahh I know baby." Karma uttered.

"You forgive me?" Jay asked.

Karma remained silent

"You don't forgive me?" Jay asked as he forcefully pushed his dick inside of Karma

"Oh shit daddy I'm cumin!" Karma screamed.

"You forgive me?" Jay asked again.

"Ahhhhhhhhhh! Oh my god!" Karma screamed as she came on his dick.

Jay still had not cum and Karma still had not answered his question. Before he could ask her again she turned around and dropped to her knees. She began to lick all of her juices off. Before Karma took all of him into her mouth Jay picked her up and laid her across the table. He slowly reinserted his dick inside of her. Jay's pushed himself inside Karma slow and steady.

"Ahh baby I'm bout to cum!" Jay said barley able to stand.

"Cum daddy" Karma looked up and naughtily said.

Before she could say another word Jay had cum inside of her.

"I forgive you."

Jay picked Karma up and carried her to their bedroom. They continued to make love for hours and hours but in the back of Jay's mind he still questioned Karma's fidelity.

PaperCut Publishing Presents….

Payback is a bitch! Karma never expected Jay to actually hit her but she honestly could not blame him. Seriously if he would have done the same disappearing act she had she would have been mad as hell too. Karma felt slightly bad for making him worry but when she thought about that night she realized he deserved it and more. The one thing she was sure of was the fact that her marriage to Jay was over. Their relationship was beyond repair because she could never trust him again. Karma was not leaving without spreading her pain and resentment. The one thing Jay loved more than her was money and by the time she was finished with him he would not have neither.

Karma used to be his bottom bitch she knew all of the in's and out's of his "business". The jewelry store was just a front for all of the illegal doings he was into. He tried to sell her that bullshit about him going legit but she never believed him. What you have to understand is that a man like Jay will never go legit because he was born, bred and raised in the streets.

He did not know anything but street life and that game was played by different rules.

One of the reasons for their connection was the fact that Karma was raised the same way. She never played, cheated or fronted on Jay ever. Karma always had his back and best interest at hand until now that is. She put up with that whole Asia fiasco and now he brings another bitch into their mix. Karma could no longer stand for the bullshit Jay dished.

Karma and Jay made love all that night and even though it felt really good it did not change anything. The same way he fucked her he had fucked someone else. Lately, they had not been using protection but Karma had been on the pill since the "Rich Mitch" days. In the past they always used condoms because Karma would always forget to take her pill. Karma had been on top of it but her period had yet to make an appearance this month. As Karma thought about it she was not sure if her period had come last month. She was so caught up in Jay's infidelity that she did not realize it.

Ironically Jay noticed as well since they had been making love daily since the infamous fight.

"Baby when you supposed to get your period?" Jay asked.

"I think it's like the sixth." Karma answered.

"Uh baby it's the twenty-sixth." Jay informed her.

"You know it comes at different times when I forget to take the birth control." Karma responded.

"Yeah but baby it's been almost two months since our fight and you haven't had one. Do you think you might be pregnant?" Jay inquired.

"No it'll probably come in a couple of days."

Jay accepted that answer and fell asleep but Karma was unable to sleep. Getting pregnant was not apart of her plan. Leaving him would be out of the question if she was pregnant with his child. Karma began thinking about how some of her habits had changed. She was sleeping a lot more and even eating more. A few weeks ago she weighed herself and noticed that she had gained five pounds. Oh no Karma thought; could she really be pregnant? She freed herself from Jay's embrace and walked downstairs. She did what she always did when in doubt and called Angel.

"Yeah" a lethargic Angel answered.

"I'm pregnant!" Karma whispered.

"What?" Angel uttered.

"I'm pregnant!" Karma shouted.

"Congratulations." Angel responded.

"What! I'm pregnant by my cheating husband. Wake the fuck up Angel." Karma yelled.

"Karma what do you want me to say? Be happy you were always worried that you couldn't have kids after the abortion. Maybe this will bring you guys back together I don't know." Angel said slightly irritated.

"He cheated on me Angel! How can I bring a child into this madness?" Karma asked trying to whisper.

"So what, look at Kobe and his wife they got over it."

"He's a millionaire she would be dumb to leave. Anyways I'm going to go the doctor tomorrow to see if I'm even pregnant before I get all crazy"

"Ok!" Angel said before hanging up.

Karma walked back upstairs and climbed into bed and cuddled next to Jay. Maybe a baby could make things better she thought before drifting off to sleep. When Karma finally awakened Jay had already left. She jumped into the shower and got dressed.

Once she made her way downstairs she noticed a note on the microwave. It read *"heat me for 1:30 and enjoy. Jay"*. Maybe this baby thing was not as bad as she had initially thought. She followed his directions and found a plate containing a ham and cheese omelet with hash browns. She walked over to the toaster and found two slices of bread waiting to be toasted. While the bread was being toasted she walked over to the refrigerator to pour some juice but of course it was already poured. Things had not been this good in a long time she contemplated.

After enjoying a luxuriating meal Karma decided it was time to face the music and call the doctor. Karma scheduled an appointment for 1:00 that afternoon. She proceeded to wash her dishes and straightened up the kitchen. Karma arrived at the doctor's office a few minutes early. There were not many people ahead of her so she did not have to wait long. The nurse called her to the back and took her to the exam room. After a few minutes Dr. Kumar entered.

"Karma it's been awhile what's going on?" he said while taking a seat on the stool.

"Well I haven't had my period in a couple of months and I think I may be pregnant." Karma bashfully said.

"Ok well lie back on the table and let's take a look."

The doctor rubbed a cold jelly substance over Karma's belly and performed an ultrasound. Karma found out that she was in fact three months pregnant. She left the doctor's office with mixed feelings. On one hand she was happy because she did not think she would be able to conceive a child. But how could she bring a baby into this madness called her life. Her husband was a cheater and he was abusive but she was still in love with him.

People say that babies are blessings so they must have done something right. The first person she called was Angel but she only got her voicemail. Karma briefly braced herself before dialing the next number. Jay answered and before he could say anything Karma blurted, "I'm pregnant."

"So what you wanna do?" Jay asked.

"Umm what do you mean?" Karma questioned.

"I'm saying is you gonna keep it?" Jay asked nonchalantly.

"Of course I'm keeping it why wouldn't I keep it. Secondly why are you coming at me like I'm one of your jump offs. Just last night you were all happy and now you're acting brand new."

"I'll talk to you when I get home." Jay said before hanging up.

What the hell was that about? Maybe he's just having a bad day at work she thought before jumping to conclusions. Or maybe he was laid up with another chick she thought as she drove home. Karma walked into the house and called her store to check on things. Her assistant manager Lisa answered and informed Karma that the day had been somewhat slow. Karma told her that she would not be in today and to call if she needed anything. After today's events Karma was tired even though it was only a little after 3:00pm. After she reached her bedroom she removed her clothing and snuggled under the covers.

The sound of voices alarmed Karma as she awakened from a deep sleep. There was a strong aroma of barbecue and she could here music playing with some laughter in the background. Karma went to the bathroom to freshen up and get dressed again. Karma had been sleeping for almost six hours straight. She threw her hair into a ponytail and applied some eyeliner and lip gloss. As she walked downstairs the music and chatting suddenly came to an abrupt halt. Karma continued down the stairs apprehensively but after reaching the last step she turned toward the living room.

"Surprise!" a room filled of family and friends screamed in unison.

Karma was still in complete shock when Jay approached her with a champagne glass filled with water. As Jay handed her a glass he asked everyone to raise their glasses.

"Karma I love you and I'm so happy that we're having our first child together. You are the best wife I could ever ask for and I know you'll be the best mom as well. The doctor said we have about six more months before he arrives so until then. Cheers!" Everyone repeated and sipped from their glasses.

Jay and Karma tapped glasses and finished their drinks as Jay wrapped his arm around her. Jay could be so unpredictable at times she thought. After their prior conversation she would have never imagined that she would have wakened up to this. At that moment she knew everything was going to be fine.

"Come on baby I know you're hungry remember you're eating for two now." Jay said as he led Karma into the kitchen.

Angel's absence was definitely the talk of the party. Karma had been so shocked by everything that she did not initially notice Angel's absence. Karma asked Jay why Angel was not in attendance and he informed her that he invited her but she did not have a babysitter. That was odd Karma thought, why didn't she just bring the kids. Karma knew something was up and she intended to find out tomorrow.

Falling

Angel felt bad for missing Karma's surprise baby announcement party. As her best friend she should have been there. Angel feared it would have been awkward since it would have been their first time together since the infamous night.

Technically Angel did not lie because her mom had been reluctant to watch the kids as of late. Angel tried to act as if that night with Karma did not mean anything. Honestly, Angel was never attracted to Karma or any female for that matter. Maybe she was just lonely because it had been awhile since she had gotten some.

Angel's personal life may have been in array but financially she had big things popping. A guy named Marlon approached her about investing into a new night club. It was a great deal but she was more interested in being a co-owner rather than an investor. He eventually agreed to Angel's terms and they were busy planning their grand opening in three weeks.

Angel's days were extremely hectic but her children were still her first priority. Madison made the honor roll and was going to receive her certificate at an assembly later that afternoon. Angel was very proud and planned on being on the front row. As a matter of fact she was going to stop by the mall and pick her daughter up something. At the mall Angel bought Madison a new Hello Kitty necklace.

Angle decided to get her truck washed before heading over to the school. Luckily, as she pulled up there was only one truck ahead of her. The car wash attendant approached the car and she purchased the "everything" package. The package included cleaning of the inside, outside and they even shinned the rims. Angel climbed out of her truck and walked inside of the car wash toward the waiting room. As she opened the door her eyes landed on a piece of art. This man was fine she felt star struck because his arms were just damn. Luckily he did not notice her staring because he was reading a magazine.

He finally looked up and said "Hello"

Angel said hello as her eyes continued to glance over his caramel frame. As she sat there she wondered if he tasted as good as he looked. As she daydreamed their wedding he finally spoke breaking her daze.

"It's supposed to be a pretty nice day huh."

"Yeah I love the summer especially after these Chi- town winters." Angel responded trying to keep her composure.

"So what's your name beautiful?" he asked.

"Angel and yours?" she responded.

"I'm Trey and I hope all of the angels in heaven are as beautiful as you are."

"Thank you." Angel said slightly blushing.

"So do you live around here?"

"No my kids go to school out here. Do you live nearby?" Angel questioned.

"Yeah my son goes to Jefferson Academy where do your children go?"

"Well it's a small world because both of my children go to Jefferson. I'm actually on my way there for an assembly." Angel informed.

"Yeah I'm going to the awards assembly too maybe we could go to lunch after."

"Well I was planning on taking my kids to Chuck E. Cheese you all are welcome to join us."

"Ok that's sounds like a plan the one on Fullerton?" Trey asked as he stood up.

"Yeah" Angel nodded.

"Well it was very nice meeting you." Trey said as he kissed her hand. "See you in a few." he said as he walked toward his truck.

Before he even reached his truck Angel had Karma on speed dial. She finally answered and she told her all about Trey and their date.

"He sounds nice but ain't it kind of soon to be involving the kids?" Karma asked.

"Damn I didn't even think of it like that."

"But it's an assembly thing I'm sure there'll be other parents with their kids there." Angel hoped.

"Yeah that's true but girl I'm going to call you back I think I"

Was all Karma could say before she began to vomit profusely. Angel had heard enough and decided to just hang up. The attendant then informed her that her truck was ready. She climbed into the truck and made her way over to the school. As she parked she noticed Trey's truck in the corner. Angel walked into the school and someone directed her towards the auditorium. The auditorium was packed but luckily she found a seat in the center near the front.

Angel always missed DeMarcus at these types of events. Seeing all of the parents together and knowing how proud he would have been made Angel sad. When she saw her baby walk across the stage to get her award Angel was full of emotion. She almost broke into a woof woof Arsenio style but withheld herself.

As the assembly concluded the parents fished out their kids. Angel mingled with a few of her children's friends and their parents but she was definitely ready to go. After talking to the teachers and parents they finally made their way outside. As they walked towards the truck she noticed Trey's truck was gone. Angel hoped he would be at Chuck E. Cheese as planned but something did not seem right. Since the two strangers did not exchange information it was now left up to fate.

The kids were overjoyed when Angel pulled into the Chuck E. Cheese parking lot. She briefly glanced over the parking lot for Trey's truck but did not see it. Maybe he was running late she thought as they walked toward the door. They stamped everyone's hands and the kids were off. Angel ordered a pizza and some chicken fingers then found a table. As she sat she began checking her e-mails on her cell phone. The food finally arrived when Angel found the kids but it was not long before they were off again.

A couple of hours had passed when her now worn out children returned. They cashed in their tickets and picked out their prizes. Four hours had passed and Angel's so called prince charming was a no show. As she got into the car she noticed a note on the windshield. Angel stepped out to grab the note. The note was actually a business card that read Treylon D. West III, CEO of Boss Incorporated.

Angel turned the card over and it read.

Sorry beautiful but something came up. Please forgive me and allow me the opportunity to make this up to you. Please call me I'm waiting:)!!! Trey.

By the time Angel stepped back into the truck the kids were already knocked out. She put his business card into her purse and drove home.

After Angel put the kids to bed she debated if she should call or make him wait. But calling could be a test because it was a little after ten. If he answers then he may not have a girl but if he does not he may be laid up. As she held the business card in one hand and the phone in the other she became nervous. She began to pace back and forth in the kitchen until she finally convinced herself to call. Angel laid the card on the counter and began to dial his number. After the phone rang four times she was about to hang up but before she could an out of breath male voice answered.

"Hello" he said out of breath.

"Trey? This is Angel did I catch you at a bad time?" Angel asked not sure of what to think.

"No, No I just finished working out. What took you so long?" he said a tad calmer.

"I wasn't sure if I should call since you stood me up."

"I'm really sorry about that but my little brother has Eplisey. The school called and I had to pick him up. He has ADHD also so he can be quite a handful sometimes. By the time I got him together it was late and my son had already fallen asleep. I did not have your number and I didn't want to stakeout the carwash so I left you a note. I do apologize though I was really looking forward to lunch" Trey explained.

Angel felt some relief from his explanation and the two strangers talked till dawn before falling asleep on each other.

Trey was known to his friends as Derrick but he used his first name not to be recognized. He was beginning to understand how Marlon could be in love with a woman like Angel. He and Angel had spoken on the phone for hours before they both fell asleep. It had been a long time since he woke up to the dial tone buzzing in his ear. Trey actually missed those days but his lover Marlon was so infatuated with Angel that he neglected the small things. She was actually a nice person and Trey was becoming slightly apprehensive about his plan. He thought if Angel had someone else in the picture maybe Marlon would see he had no chance.

Trey and Marlon had been an item for two years. Everything was going well up until the last six months when Angel came into the picture. Trey and Marlon lived their lives as straight men there was nothing about them that said "gay." The two lovers never held hands or showed affection in public but behind closed doors was another story.

Marlon was a successful real estate developer while Trey was a real estate broker. Trey had been living the "down low" lifestyle for almost twelve years but he was Marlon's first. Their friendship was initially an "I will scratch your back if you scratch mine" partnership but later that became literally. Marlon was beginning to rethink his lifestyle with Trey. He wanted to live a "normal" life and have a family. Marlon was so intrigued and smitten by Angel that he could no longer foresee a place for Trey. He had not cut Trey completely off but if he won Angel he was sure to.

Trey was in love with Marlon and did not want to end their affair. He could not understand why Marlon wanted to solely by with Angel. Trey decided that if Marlon wanted to end their tryst he would do so without Angel. Marlon had been with other women but Angel was the only one to make him question their relationship. Trey planned to secretly win over Angel and push her as far away from

Marlon's arms as possible. He was not sure of his approach until by coincidence he ran into Angel at the carwash. The stars in the sky had lined up perfectly he thought. After talking to Angel he realized she was a nice person but all was fair in love and war.

Marlon paced his office thinking about what Angel had just told him. It was the day he dreaded but knew was imminent. Angel had finally met someone and from the sounds of it she was very excited. At that moment Marlon wanted to come clean and confess his feelings for her but he could not. He had been going back and forth with himself on what to do about Derrick. He had feelings for him but his feelings for Angel were greater.

Recently Marlon decided he was going to leave Derrick alone for good. But now that Angel was into someone else he worried that she could reject him. Marlon had to make a move and quick. Marlon sat at his desk and stared at the blank e-mail on his monitor. He finally typed in the subject line *I love you.* Marlon poured his heart into the e-mail. He explained how much he loved and adored the recipient. Marlon shared some of their great moments but explained him and Derrick's relationship was over.

As Trey read the e-mail his heart began to break. At that moment he realized it was no longer a game or fantasy he was actually in love with Marlon. Trey had to get Marlon back and to do that he had to take Angel. He sent Angel flowers daily and surprised her with different trinkets. They dined at the finest restaurants and shopped at the most expensive boutiques. Trey made love to Angel but fantasized of Marlon. He was ready to up the ante and take their relationship to the next level. He was already playing daddy to Angel's children it was now time to move in.

Guess Who

Angel and Karma's friendship had hit a shaky spot but the two friends recovered. Angel was in town for Karma's baby shower. Karma was now thirty-one weeks pregnant. Angel was finishing up the last minute details for the party when Karma called. Karma and Angel met for lunch at the Ivy. Karma looked so beautiful with child she had that glow. Angel could not believe how big Karma had gotten. She tried not to make it obvious as Karma walked toward the table.

"You don't have to stare I know I'm huge." Karma said exhausted.

"Whatever girl you look beautiful." Angel said as she hugged her best friend.

The waiter came over and took their orders.

"Angel I called you here because I don't know what to do. Remember when I told you me and Jay were receiving prank phone calls on the house and business phones?" Angel nodded as Karma continued. "Well now it's happening on Jay's cell phone at all times of the night. Last night I answered his phone and it was a woman. She told me that she and Jay were engaged. She claimed to not have known about me until last week when he told her about the baby. She came up with this plan to get back at Jay but I don't know." Karma explained.

"Who is she? Is she the girl from before?" Angel asked.

"I don't think so because the girl from before knew about me and this chick claims not to."

"I don't know she could be lying chicks these days are dirty." Angel replied.

"Yeah you're right I'm supposed to meet her later today to go over the plan. I guess we'll see."

Karma stated just before the waiter came back with their meals.

"You're going by yourself with some woman you don't even know from Eve. I'm coming with you." Angel stated.

"No I told her I would come alone but you already know I got my 22 aka pinky as back up." Karma said as she pointed toward her purse.

"Oh ok well make sure you call me before and after you get there." Angel said while cutting her salad.

"Of course anyway tell me about this Trey." Karma inquired.

"Well he's a real estate broker tall, dark and chocolate. He likes kids and he has one son. His son's mom died during child birth which means no baby mama drama. He's everything I've been looking for in a man. Trey makes me feel like the ultimate queen. He wines, dines and spoils me like a baby. On top of that the kids love him I really think he's the one. We've been talking about getting a place together but it's only been four months." Angel gushed.

"Damn he sounds perfect you know I'm the wrong person to talk about timing. Me and Jay became an item, got engaged and married all in the same day."

Both friends burst into laughter at Karma's statement. They finished their meals and went their separate ways. Angel went shopping while Karma went to meet her husband's girlfriend. Karma was supposed to meet Cheryl in the McDonald's inside of Wal-Mart.

Karma walked through McDonald's looking for someone wearing a red dress. Karma was about to turn around before she saw a familiar face. There sat a brown-skinned woman wearing a red fitted dress but she was no stranger. She was the woman from that night. Karma would never forget that night or her face. Karma slowly approached the woman and introduced herself.

Cheryl divulged the details to her plan of the ultimate revenge. Karma agreed but Jay was not the only one she was going to get revenge on. As soon as Karma reached her truck she called Angel and told her everything on her drive home. Jay greeted Karma with a kiss on her cheek and one onto her stomach as she walked inside. Karma just stared at Jay because she knew he had no clue what he was in store for.

This is some bullshit Jay thought as he gazed over naked pictures of himself having sex with Cheryl. He knew Cheryl was crazy but he did not know it was to this extent. Jay had fallen out with Cheryl before but in the past they had always gotten back together. He missed Cheryl but with the baby on the way he did not want to take any chances of getting caught. Jay repeatedly called Cheryl's phone but her voicemail kept picking up.

Her letter requested $50,000 in cash to be placed in a safety deposit box in National City Bank. The letter also stated if the money was not delivered by 3:00 Friday duplicates would be sent to his wife's home and boutique. Jay did not believe Cheryl knew where he lived nor where his wife's boutique was located but he could not take the chance. It was now noon and he only had three hours to deliver the money. The money was not a problem but hiding the missing $50,000 from Karma would be the difficult part.

Jay decided to use the cash from his safe at home. The only problem was Karma was due any day now and she was not suppose to go anywhere. Jay then decided to take the money out of his jewelry store account. Jay did not inform Isaac because he thought it was a one time event. He believed he could take the money and replace it before Isaac even noticed. But what Jay didn't know was this was one of many payments to come.

Jay delivered the money to the safety deposit box as instructed. He called Cheryl but there was no answer and he did not leave a message. Jay believed Cheryl had gotten what she wanted and would probably leave him alone.

Angel was really falling for Trey but she was not sure if she was ready to take it to the next level. Trey was becoming very persistent about getting a place together. Angel was really feeling him but was she ready to leave behind what she and DeMarcus built. He had worked very hard to purchase her house and to ensure that his girls never had to depend on no man. Angel was sure DeMarcus expected her to move on but was she moving too fast?

Angel was on her way to meet Trey for dinner where she was supposed to give him her decision. For the entire day Angel went back and forth between the idea and she was still deadlocked. It was not a specific reason why she should not but something kept making her reluctant.

As she arrived at Morton's of Chicago she had to make a decision. Trey was a good man and her children absolutely adored him. It would be nice to wake up next to someone again. There would be no more lonely nights she thought. As Angel stepped out of the vehicle she had finally come to a decision. The valet handed her the ticket and proceeded to drive off as she walked inside.

"Hello, I'm meeting Treylon West is he already here." Angel inquired.

"Um yes he is right this way." the hostess instructed.

Trey stood and passionately kissed Angel on the cheek. The couple ordered wine and a spinach & artichoke dip as an appetizer. As they waited for their food there was an eerie silence between the two. They were both nervous until Trey broke the silence.

"So are we going to be roomies or what?" Trey asked.

"Yeah I guess so are you sure you want to I can be a little messy." Angel smirked somewhat taken aback by his humor.

"Are you sure because baby I love you and I want to spend the rest of my life with you."

Before Angel could react to his words she looked up to find him on one knee. There he stood with a small ring box peering into Angel's eyes. Nearby patrons stared on waiting for Angel to respond. She looked around then reluctantly said, "Yes".

"Yes, yes I'll marry you." Angel said as she hugged Trey.

The onlookers began to applaud as the happy couple toasted to their engagement. After finishing dinner the happy couple went back to Angel's home to make love without any restrictions. Nothing was out of bounds they did every freaky thing possible as their fluids intertwined the couple became one.

The Big Payback

Karma was supposed to be on bed rest per her doctor's orders. But she was craving some southwestern spring rolls from Chilis. It took her forever to get down the stairs but once she made it to the garage she was in business. As soon as Karma merged onto the freeway she began feeling cramps in her stomach area. She assumed the baby was just hungry so she continued to Chilis.

Karma finally arrived at Chilis but as she stepped out of the truck liquid dripped down her legs. Oh my God Karma thought she was about to have the baby. Pain suddenly hit her cervix as she tried to walk toward the patio. A dining customer rushed to her side and screamed for help. He brought her a chair to sit in while they waited for the ambulance.

The nice gentleman said his name was Paul and for Karma not to worry. He was actually in medical school and could tell that Karma still had some ways to go. Paul reassured Karma that she was not going to have her baby in Chilis walkway. He also called Jay once the ambulance arrived and told him what hospital they were going to.

As Jay was leaving National City Bank he received a call that Karma was going into labor. This was the last thing he needed right now. Jay was beginning to succumb to the pressure. Cheryl was still blackmailing him but the stakes kept growing bigger. He had already given her close to $600,000 over the course of two months. The money was becoming more difficult to hide from Isaac and even Karma was asking questions. Jay summed up the missing money to bad investments but that excuse was not going to last long. Jay decided he was not going to pay any more money. He had no way of contacting Cheryl because her phone was disconnected but he was done paying.

Jay walked into the hospital with the world on his shoulders. He was excited about the baby but with him not paying Cheryl how long would happiness exist inside of his home. The nurse directed Jay to Karma's room. When Jay walked into the room the doctor was administering Karma's epidural. Karma looked to be in extreme pain. Jay walked over to hold his wife's hand. The doctor stated that Karma was about 4-5 centimeters dilated. He insisted that it would not be long before the baby was there.

Within an hour Jay Raylon Stevenson II was welcomed into the world. The proud parents took turns holding their new bundle of joy. At that moment it seemed everything they had gone through was worth it. Jay was no longer concerned with Cheryl he was finally content.

Karma stayed in the hospital for three days before she and the baby were released. Jay attended to

Karma's every need and/or want. The baby had brought back a spark that had been missing from before.

Little J.R. was turning four months old this weekend. Jay planned a romantic evening for him and his wife. It was their first date since the baby had arrived. The couple dined at a new restaurant in downtown New Jersey called Antonio's Bistro. Karma was very paranoid about leaving the baby with a stranger. She checked in with the nanny every half and hour. Finally Jay convinced her to relax and after a few glasses of wine she did.

The two lovebirds walked the pier and eventually ended up making love on the beach until dawn. They were awakened by the sun when panic overcame Karma. She searched for her phone inside of her purse. Karma finally found her phone and she had twenty-three missed calls. Before she could dial out the nanny was already calling her again.

"Mrs. Stevenson he's gone J.R. is gone. I went to give him his breakfast but he wasn't in his crib." the nanny screamed hysterically.

"What do you mean J.R. is gone. What have you done?" Karma said as she and Jay ran to their car.

"Oh my god where is my baby? Why would someone do this?" Karma cried.

Within fifteen minutes Jay and Karma pulled up to their home. They were met by three New Jersey squad cars. The police asked for Jay and Karma to go down to the police department. They were subjected to four hours of grueling questions. The police finally issued a Amber's alert but there were no witnesses and as of 8:00 that evening no one had yet responded to the alert.

Jay and Karma were completely distraught for different reasons. Jay was worried that his affair with Cheryl would come up. The police already considered the parents as the first suspects. With the blackmail, money and affair he was a sure suspect with a motive. Karma felt guilty for being selfish and leaving her baby alone with a stranger. She kept telling herself that it was too soon to leave him.

A week had passed and J.R. had yet to be found. Spectators were saying the chances of finding J.R. alive were slim to none. Jay and Karma did not believe the hype. Angel came to support her best friend but she could not imagine what her friend was going through. Karma barely ate or slept since J.R.'s kidnapping. The police had no definite motive behind the kidnapping but they suspected that a ransom of some sort may be in demand. The police rummaged through numerous dead end tips without any prospects.

The kidnapping and investigation was beginning to take a toll on Jay and Karma's relationship. Karma resented him for cheating and faulted him for their son's disappearance.

Cheryl watched the news as the city was in an uproar about an abducted young boy. It infuriated her how the news depicted Jay and Karma. They acted as if they were the All American family instead of the Soprano's like they actually were. Cheryl turned all of her focus back to Jay and how concerned he appeared. Full of disgust Cheryl reminisced on her rocky relationship with Jay over the last year and a half.

Cheryl and Jay actually met when Jay and Isaac were looking for locations for their New Jersey jewelry store. At the time Cheryl was the personal assistant to a major real estate broker. She had no real interest in real estate but it paid the bills. That was until her boss met up with the handsome yet suave Mr. Stevenson. Cheryl was instantly attracted to his professional yet street creditable image. In the beginning they were all business because Jay was in a relationship.

Cheryl did not set out to become a home wrecker so to speak but she fell in love with Jay. Cheryl would listen to him as he would vent about the problems within his relationship. She wondered how any woman could not appreciate a man of his stature. Cheryl had developed so much hate and resentment toward Karma over time it became personal. She hated that Jay was so infatuated with a woman who did not appreciate him as she would. Cheryl did not intend on hurting anyone she was in fact saving Jay from a lifetime of misery. Everything he needed Cheryl was and everything he wanted she had.

Jay appreciated Cheryl but he was in love with Karma. In his eyes Cheryl did not have anything on his wife. It was like comparing a steak um to filet mignon both are good but they are worlds apart.

Jay hooking up with Cheryl was a case of too much Patron at the wrong time. He had just finished arguing with Karma before he went to have a drink with Cheryl. His frustration turned one drink into ten or eleven. Jay was drunk beyond belief and as a friend Cheryl advised him to sleep on her couch at least until the morning. Jay stumbled up her stairs and plopped down on the couch. His vision was in and out but when he saw Cheryl standing in front of him naked with just her heels on he instantly sat up.

"Um wha what are you doin?" Jay said trying to keep his composure.

"What you've been wanting." Cheryl said seductively.

"Cheryl you look good. I mean really good but I can't do this. I love Karma too much for this." Jay said.

Cheryl bent down in between Jay's legs and unbuckled his belt. She then unbuttoned and unzipped his pants without any protest from Jay. Cheryl then slowly inserted his member into her mouth. She slowly sucked his member until he could no longer take anymore. Cheryl stood up and straddled his rock hard dick and covered it with her drenching pussy. She rode his dick for only five minutes before he exploded inside of her.

Jay was unable to stand from all of the alcohol but he still wanted to get Cheryl from the back. Cheryl assumed the position on all fours while Jay stood on his knees behind her. He inserted his dick again unprotected. Jay was about to come inside her again but this time Cheryl turned around to catch his semen.

No matter how much Jay told himself it was wrong he could not stop. Cheryl had completely turned him out. She did things no woman had ever done to him. Jay had ejaculated on every part of Cheryl's body from her mouth to her ass. Cheryl was completely no holds bar in the bedroom. Jay had been intoxicated the first night but it did not take much for round two.

Jay and Cheryl's relationship was mutually sexual but things changed when Jay moved to New Jersey permanently. Cheryl was becoming more attached and clingy. She was becoming more and more jealous of his relationship with his wife. Eventually Jay broke off the relationship completely because of her obsessive ways. Jay had no idea of the lengths Cheryl would go through to get him back.

The Stock Exchange

Jay and Karma finally received the phone call they had both hoped and dreaded for. The kidnappers called for ransom. It had been seventeen days since they had kidnapped J.R.. The kidnappers asked for $500,000 in cash and ten kilos of cocaine. Jay persuaded Karma not to mention the dope to the police. The request for cocaine made both Jay and Karma leery. Jay feared that Karma would find out that he was not completely legit. It had been years since he had actually touched dope but he was very much still involved in the business.

Over the years Jay had burned many bridges and had fired many disgruntle employees. For someone to be as ruthless as to kidnap his newborn son he must have done something severe. Jay thought about all of the people he had done wrong. There was Asia, Cheryl and some other jump offs but they could not be capable of something like this he thought.

Jay pushed the thought out of his head and focused on how he was going to obtain ten kilos. It would have been effortless to retrieve that kind of weight before the blackmailing began but now was another story. Jay spent a lot of money for the blackmail and a lot covering the blackmail. Fortunately, he did not have to worry about getting the cash for the ransom because the police were going to handle that.

Jay called Isaac and filled him in on the situation. Isaac was sympathetic to the situation but he also informed Jay that he had some concerns. Jay's body froze instantly as Isaac spoke. Jay believed he was finally caught with his hand in the cookie jar.

"Look man I know a guy that would front you the weight but what's really going on. I was looking over the bank statements and there have been a lot of withdrawals and transfers from our account." Isaac spoke calmly.

"Remember when I was telling you that new company was fucking up? Man all of our orders been wrong; they either coming in late or just wrong all together. They even were billing us for the wrong shit. I've had to go through their receipts with a fine tooth comb. Nah mean. When I get J.R. back I'm going to focus on getting that shit together. I just can't focus with everything going on." Jay explained praying that Isaac would take his weak excuse.

Fortunately, Isaac did not argue but he sure as hell did not fall for the bullshit Jay tried to feed him. Isaac believed every dog had its day and Jay would reap if was playing him. Unbeknown to Jay Isaac had a plan of his own.

Karma could no longer take the waiting game. She decided to go to Down Bottom and let work get her mind off of things. As Karma walked toward her store a familiar face stood by its entrance.

"What are you doing here?" Karma asked.

"That's how you greet an old friend." The familiar acquaintance responded. Before Karma could respond they continued. "I've come to get what I'm owed. You up here living the fabulous life and I'm still in the hood. I'm the fuckin reason why you got this life. I've come to collect my cut."

"Cut of what all this shit is in Jay's name my name ain't on shit." Karma stated.

"Bitch do I look stupid. Yall are fuckin married what's his is yours. Don't try to play me like that I know you and you ain't stupid." she said as she reached for Karma.

"Get the fuck outta here with that. That shit was years ago. I was young back then that shit ain't even relevant anymore." Karma said irritated.

"Moving on to more relevant issues I know everything and I want my cut. I've been watching you for months Miss. Karma."

"What the fuck are you talking about?" Karma said distancing herself from the assailant.

"Oh so now you wanna play dumb. Well does Jay know Angel's been living up here for the last three months? Karma said nothing as the woman continued. "I wondered why a wife wouldn't tell her husband her best friend was in town? You finally found out about Cheryl huh? It's all starting to become so very clear Karma. If I was able to figure it out you don't think the police will?"

"Look what do you want? The police are watching our finances. There's nothing I can give you right now." Karma lied.

"Well give me some of that blackmail money." the woman countered.

"Look I don't know what the fuck you talking bout or what the fuck you want but I ain't on it. Jay fell for your bullshit not me so please get from in front of my establishment." Karma said walking toward her front door."

"Alright well tell Cheryl I said what's up."

"Asia wait, look I'll give you $120,000 but all I got is $60,000 right now." Karma pleaded.

"I knew your ass would be singing another tune." Asia said with a smirk as she walked into Down Bottom.

Karma walked Asia back to her office and revealed her and Cheryl's plan of revenge. What Karma did not expect was for Asia to unveil some things of her own. Asia told Karma how Jay had been messing with her and Cheryl while he was with Karma. Karma was shocked but she was not too sure of what to believe. What she did know was that Asia could not be trusted. Karma knew Asia was dangerous and she had to move with caution. Karma wondered how Asia could know so much but she knew Asia was crazy from Jay's old stories.

Cheryl was pissed from the phone call she just received from Karma. There was suddenly a third person in on the kidnapping. That meant one less cut of the ransom. This was bullshit Cheryl thought as she held little J.R.. Fuck Karma Cheryl spat as she packed her belongings. Fuck the plan she was going to take little J.R. and make her own family. Cheryl loaded up her car and was on her way. Cheryl needed to make a move so she called Jay.

"Yeah" Jay answered.

"You wanna see your son again?" Cheryl questioned.

"What the fuck? Is this you Cheryl? I swear to God Cheryl if you took my son I'm gonna kill you." Jay screamed.

"Look all that bullshit isn't going to get your son back so what is it?"

"What the fuck you mean of course I want my son you crazy bitch." Jay yelled.

"What's with all the name calling your wife is what got you into all of this mess anyway?" Cheryl informed.

"What the fuck. Leave my wife out of this. Look you crazy bitch where the fuck is my son."

"Look I ain't gon be too many more crazy bitches. If you want to see your son you need to meet me at Macy's in Time Square by 8:00."

"What the hell Time Square? It's fuckin' rush hour I'll never make it by eight." Jay explained.

"Well me and J.R. have an 11:35 flight so if you're not there oh well. Also don't tell that conniving wife or the cops if you wanna see J.R. again." Cheryl stated before pressing end.

The next call Cheryl placed was to another disposable phone carrier.

Jay was completely stunned he had no idea Cheryl was capable of such a thing. It was now ten minutes after six and Jay had less than two hours to get to Time Square in New York City. He immediately hopped into his truck and headed for the highway. Jay wanted to call Karma and let her know J.R. was ok but that would open the door up for too many questions.

Jay drove speedily down Highway 9 until traffic came to an abrupt standstill at the New Jersey toll. Inch by inch Jay finally made it to the toll booth. He paid his toll but traffic was still stop and go. Finally the traffic began to break but he now only had 45 minutes to meet Cheryl. Jay swerved far to the right and drove down the shoulder. As Jay flew passed stopped traffic he failed to notice the unmarked vehicle that had been following him since he left work.

It was now 8:36 and Jay was just pulling around to Times Square. Jay pulled up to the curb and began walking toward Macy's. As he walked he looked for Cheryl and J.R. but he did not see them anywhere.

Times Square was never dull but today it seemed to be extra packed. As he glanced up he spotted Brittany Spears performing on the big screen near the MTV studios. Damn he thought of all days to come down here. Jay finally made his way inside Macy's but it was now five minutes till nine.

Ride or Die

Angel jumped into the cab as she left the O'Hara Airport. It had been over a month since she last seen Trey. The two had been having phone sex on the regular but Angel knew that Trey was going crazy inside. She decided she would surprise him for the weekend.

After about a twenty minute ride the yellow cab pulled alongside her tree lawn. As she pulled up she noticed the garage door was open. She paid the cab driver and ran up the driveway. As Angel walked into the garage she noticed the door was cracked. She quietly walked inside and slowly walked upstairs.

An eerie feeling came over her as she walked toward her bedroom. Nothing could have prepared Angel for what she was about to walk in on.

"What the fuck!" Angel screamed.

Trey jumped up with his dick still inside of Marlon's mouth.

"Trey, Marlon, what the fuck! Oh my God"

Was all Angel managed to say as she backed out of her bedroom. Marlon ran toward her trying to explain. But what could he explain? How could he explain Trey's dick being inside of his mouth? On top of that why were they inside of her bedroom? She stumbled backwards almost falling down the stairs. Marlon reached for her arm but Angel quickly snatched her arm back. Angel lost her footing and began to tumble down the stairs.

"Angel!" Marlon screamed as he rushed down the stairs.

Trey stood at the top of the stairs with a smirk on his face. He could not have planned things anymore perfectly. Trey had originally planned to e-mail Angel pictures from Marlon's old Black Planet account. But Angel walking in on them took the cake. She would never take Marlon back he thought.

"Angel is you ok?" Marlon asked as he reached the last step.

"Get the fuck away from me. Don't touch me! Angel screamed.

"Ok I'll stay right here are you hurt?" Marlon questioned.

"What the fuck you ain't got nothing to say. You just proposed to me. I let you around my kids. You nasty muthafucka I should kill you." Angel screamed as she scooted toward the kitchen.

"You see Marlon was mine first and I'm sorry but I told you I don't like to share." Trey said as he casually walked down the stairs. "Actually Angel it was you who set all of this up. When you told me Marlon was going to bring some papers by I knew I had to make a move. I left the garage door opened as I hid in the back. Marlon did as I predicted and walked right inside. I knocked on the door like an uninvited guest."

"Derrick you're Trey?" Marlon asked confused.

"Yup I'm the nigga that took your bitch. You should take note her head game is off the chain. The same way I cum in your mouth I ca"

Before Trey could finish he was now facing the barrel of Marlon's gun.

"Nigga put that gun down you ain't gon use it." Trey spat.

"Shut the fuck up! You did this to me I wasn't like this before I met you. You turned me out but you won't turn out anyone else." Marlon said before pulling the trigger six times.

Pop, Pop, Pop, Pop, Pop, Pop, Pop, and Pop!

Angel hobbled toward her purse to retrieve her cell phone. She picked it up and dialed 911.

"911 what's your emergency?

"I just killed an intruder please send someone. Angel calmly spoke.

"Are you hurt? Is the intruder still alive?" the operator asked.

"No he is dead."

"Is anyone else injured?" the operator questioned.

"Yes my fiancé. He killed my fiancé." Angel began to sob.

"Ok just hang in there help is on the way." the operator assured before disconnecting.

Jay had searched every inch of Macy's before giving up hope. It was now almost ten o'clock before he walked out of Macy's. As he walked through the doors a familiar voice interrupted his trance.

"Your two hours late I thought you loved lil J.R.." Cheryl taunted.

"Bitch I swear to God if you've done anything to my son I will"

"Save that shit for the birds where's my money?" Cheryl inquired.

"Look the police was suppose to give us the money but we can pick up the keys right now." Jay informed.

"Naw fuck that I need the cash." Cheryl countered.

"Look if I get the cash the police are gonna trace it so let's just go get the keys and give me my damn son." Jay explained becoming impatient.

"Alright" Cheryl replied.

Jay and Cheryl walked toward where Jay's vehicle was parked but it was no longer there. It had been parked in a no parking zone and had been towed. Jay did not know what he was thinking by parking there because in New York City they did not play when it came to parking. Jay called Isaac to see what was up with the keys. Isaac said he was sending a guy up there to meet him and Cheryl in about ten minutes.

Jay and Cheryl sat on the bench in complete silence. As they sat a squad car sped passed them. Then three more followed which did not startle Jay and Cheryl they were in New York City. It would have been more startling to not hear sirens or gun shots. Two men wearing suits were walking in their direction. Jay was beginning to think that Cheryl may have set him up. If the two men would have gotten any closer Jay was going to make a run for it.

"Freeze put your hands where I can see them."

"Huh what's going on I didn't do nothing." Jay spoke.

"This is the New York City police we have you surrounded." the other suit stated.

As Jay lifted his hands he looked around and saw cops everywhere. Plain dressed cops and uniform cops were indeed surrounding him. There were even sharp shooters on top of the building across the street.

"This is a misunderstanding this woman has been blackmailing me. She kidnapped my son and that's why I am here." Jay tried to explain as he was being handcuffed.

"You are under arrest for the kidnapping and ransom attempt of a minor, drug trafficking, blackmail and tax invasion." the officer said before reading Jay his rights.

A female officer searched Cheryl before placing her under arrest as well. The officer read Cheryl her rights then handcuffed her too. Both officers walked the two suspects toward separate squad cars.

"Where's my son Cheryl? Where the fuck is my son?" Jay screamed.

"Your son has been safely returned to your wife." the officer nonchalantly said.

"What! What the fuck is going on?" Jay asked as he was guided into the squad car.

Karma

Karma watched as Jay and Cheryl were arrested. She felt no remorse as she held onto her son tightly. She sincerely hoped that one day J.R. would forgive her.

Karma was crushed when she found out that Jay was cheating on her. She and Angel had devised the ultimate plan of revenge. Karma planned to blackmail Jay with pictures from the video she had taken of him with Cheryl. She initially was just going to get the money and leave it until the prank calls started. When she found out Cheryl actually lied about who she was Karma elevated her plan.

When Karma met with Cheryl they came up with the whole kidnapping scenario. Karma was initially worried that Cheryl would harm J.R. but Angel reassured her J.R. would be ok. When Asia came back into the picture Karma was reluctant to continue with the kidnapping scheme. But when Angel went back home it became a perfect opportunity to kill two birds with one stone.

Karma called Isaac in the beginning of the blackmail because she knew what Jay would do. She knew Jay was afraid to take the money from their account so that only left the business. Instead of keeping the money she put it in an account under his name which was eventually turned over to the cops. Karma told Cheryl to leave J.R. in a rental car inside a parking garage where Asia would be waiting. Once Asia had J.R. Karma called Cheryl to go meet up with Jay. The next call Karma made was to the police and since Jay was their main suspect it was an easy story to sell.

Angel walked out of the third district police department where Karma, Asia, J.R., Madison and Mason waited. She still could not believe that she was walking away as a free woman. Angel told the police Marlon was embezzling money from their business. When she decided to end their partnership he was livid and came to her house to confront her. She was not at home and a fight ensued between Marlon and her fiancé. Angel walked in on the fight and tried to break it up which is when Marlon pushed her down the stairs.

Angel told them she had lost conscious for awhile and all that she remembered was Marlon shooting her fiancé. She told them she had no recollection of shooting Marlon. According to the police Angel was indeed the victim. Who would have suspected that Angel's fiancé and business partner were lovers?

"Will the defendant please rise? You have been convicted of two counts of A-2 Felony possession of narcotics with the intent to sale, racketeering, the kidnapping and ransom attempt of a minor, drug trafficking, blackmail and tax invasion. The district attorney and the jury were both very merciful to you; coincidence or not you should thank them.

The jury thinks you are a misguided young man but believes with the right guidance you could be rehabilitated. Unlike them I come across your kind everyday. You are scum and even though it could not be proven today I know you are one of the leaders in the Javier Cartel.

I also believe you did murder those two cops as well as smuggle drugs into the United States. Even though you were initially facing life in prison I am only able to give the state maximum for the charges you were convicted for.

By the power invested in me by the state of New Jersey I hereby sentence you to no more than 15 years but no less than 8 years to be served in a maximum-security correctional facility. I also render the defendant to pay the court a total of $1.5 million dollars in restitution, which is the maximum in the state of New Jersey. Court is adjourned."

Karma remained frozen on the court bench for what seemed like hours. She was unable to hear the screams and sighs all she could hear was the judge saying no less than eight years, eight fucking years and $1.5 million dollars. Their house in Newark, their cars, their bank accounts and credit cards were all depleted. Everything she owned and even her husband was considered state property.

Jay stood there in complete shock pleased and disappointed at the same time. On one hand he had gotten off like a fat rat but on the other hand eight years was a long time. He wondered if Karma would still be down for him. She had stayed down for him when he was locked up before but that was for only 27 months.

Karma seemed to believe that he was not involved in the kidnapping and had been very supportive of him since the trial. However, how could he ask her with a straight face to put her life on hold because he fucked up? And what about his son, J.R. did not deserve this life; he never even asked to be here Jay thought.

Jay glanced over at Karma and felt even worse. She sat there with no movement in complete silence as if there was no more life inside of her. She was the mother of his child and the only person he truly loved more than himself.

It felt as if time had stopped but then suddenly Karma's heart began to race as she peered over at Jay and their eyes finally met. She could feel the hurt in his eyes but he had gotten everything he deserved. Karma watched as the bailiff approached Jay before she began to walk toward him.

Jay watched Karma approach him but he quickly turned away. He could not face her or what she had to say. The seriousness in her face and the desperation in her expression made Jay very nervous.

As soon as Karma reached him the bailiff was beginning to take him away. But before he was taken Karma finally spoke.

"I knew about everything. I knew about Cheryl, the money and even Asia. I loved you with all of my heart why Jay never mind don't answer that." Karma said before handing Jay his last picture of his wife and son.

"Treasure it because it's over." Karma said before turning and walking away.

Karma did not even give Jay an opportunity to respond nor did she wait for his reaction. Karma wanted to turn around and see the look on his face but she did not. Karma finally left the courtroom and made her way to the car where Asia, Angel, J.R., Madison and Mason waited. Jay had no idea that he had just gotten played. Karma was indeed a bitch!!

www.ingramcontent.com/pod-product-compliance
Lightning Source LLC
LaVergne TN
LVHW090942080826
845145LV00003B/862

* 9 7 8 0 5 7 8 0 2 8 5 0 7 *